Murphy entered c... ...
battles, men coolly took aim, paced their shots, and squeezed the rounds off. Hogwash.

It never happened that way. When it came it was fast and tight and dirty, with smoke and noise and the flat metallic taste-smell of fear and death in your mouth, quick breathing, and trying to get as many bullets in the air at once.

And this time was no exception. The stranger in the fight at the card table heard Murphy yell, and he turned, drew his pistol, and fired. Murphy saw the smoke only after the bullet was already gone, tugging at his head when it passed through his hat brim. Because he was soft, thinking of quitting, Murphy didn't react until the man had shot twice more.

Twice more the man fired, twice the bullets passed Murphy, the last one actually rubbing his belt as the stranger tried to hit him.

Tried to kill him.

He's trying to kill me.

All fast then. Murphy fell to the right and fired as fast as he could, three times, but the first round did it. The bullet took the man almost exactly in the center of the sternum, and he went back and down, dying. Murphy began to straighten but no, not yet, he thought.

And as he thought it, the door to the crib room overhead opened. . . .

DISCARD

Gary Paulsen

MURPHY

POCKET BOOKS

New York   London   Toronto   Sydney   Tokyo

POCKET BOOKS, a division of Simon & Schuster, Inc.
1230 Avenue of the Americas, New York, N.Y. 10020

Copyright © 1987 by Gary Paulsen
Cover artwork copyright © 1988 Peter Caras

Published by arrangement with Walker and Company
Library of Congress Catalog Card Number: 86-15969

ISBN: 0-671-64432-7

First Pocket Books printing February 1988

10 9 8 7 6 5 4 3 2 1

POCKET and colophon are trademarks of Simon & Schuster, Inc.

Printed in U.S.A.

MURPHY

CHAPTER 1

THEY CALLED HIM sheriff or the law or sometimes things he didn't like to think about or hear. But he had the job largely because nobody else wanted it. Al Murphy, sheriff of Cincherville, Colorado, was a big man who reminded people of a bear. He had round shoulders and the almost awkward motion of a strong man who was careful but who, when he had to move fast, was surprising. Not quick so much as sure, so that when he did something, hit something, it was hit and done right.

He was originally from New York City, had been born and raised in the hell of the Tenderloin by a mother who had other things on her mind and by many, many fathers. In 1868, when Murphy was a boy, a recruiter with shiny brass buttons and a blue uniform had come through and fed him half a bucket of warm saloon beer laced with straight jack whiskey and had signed him on to head west with the cavalry and fight Indians. Of course it was all bull, Murphy found, but he didn't know that when he signed. He had pictures in his head of horses and charges from prints he had seen of the Civil War; pictures of himself slashing down red savages with a saber to save immigrant wagon trains; pictures of chevrons on his sleeve and fair-haired wagon girls looking up to him. All bull.

He never fought an Indian. He spent all his time polishing brass—Lord, he must have polished more than a ton of brass—and cleaning up horse crap like the rest of the poor lads who signed big and strong on the line.

But the army took him west to Fort Leaven-worth, Kansas. It got him out of the Tenderloin. And that counted for something. On a day when things were going wrong he crossed a crut-mean corporal named Hackner, and they fought; Murphy left the army that night, left in the dark, and Hackner spent the rest of his life in a chair with a broken back.

Murphy headed west with an army horse and saddle, a .45-70 rifle, three dollars, and nineteen bullets. Figured he had the world by the tail, he thought now, sitting in his office looking out on the dusty street. Had it all and he headed west for gold.

Now he was thirty-two, the gold was all gone, it was 1889, and he was the sheriff of Cincherville, a cratered town built on the edge of the mountains, populated by three hundred people and a miner now and then who moved through picking up anything that shined. Murphy's gold was sixty-four dollars a month, a bed in Harry's where he just had room to hang his hat if he didn't turn around, and an occasional steak at Midge's Cafe.

My gold, he thought. He shook his leg a bit. He was leaning back, his feet up on the table that served for a desk, and his left leg had gone to sleep. He stood and limped back and forth to push the needles out. When his leg was working normally he poured himself a cup of cold coffee. He liked cold coffee because it cut the dust of the street out of his mouth. He liked anything that cut out any part of the street.

Somebody at the Red Ram had told him once—probably over double shots—that poor circulation meant you were getting old. He wondered if thirty-two was old. Depends, he thought, on how strong the drunk is you're slugging and throwing in the cell. Sometimes he felt old. Really old.

He heard raucous coughing in the back where he had two cells. They were really only strap iron bolted into two cages, with cots and buckets in the corner. Murphy poured more coffee and went to the back. One of the cells was empty, in the other a man was leaning over a bucket vomiting and hacking.

"You feel something round and furry come up

swallow quick . . ." He didn't finish the joke. Clyde had heard all the drink-and-puke jokes in the world. "Here. I brought you some coffee."

Clyde Parker turned from the bucket. His eyes were red and bulging from the push-strain, and his shirt was covered with old vomit. "Coffee, hell. I need a bottle."

"No. You don't. Take it, it's on the house."

Clyde took the cup, shook half of it out before it got to his mouth, swallowed the other half, and barely made it back to the bucket where he threw it back up, with interest. Soon he was in the dry heaves, at last he stood and turned, in partial control. "God."

"He won't help." Murphy took the key from the wall and unlocked the cell door. "Get the mop and bucket and clean the cell out. Then you can go. The fine is five dollars, pay when you can."

Clyde moved slowly, got the mop and bucket and started to work on the cell.

Murphy went back out into the office. He sat at his desk again, propped up his feet, and looked out the window. It was midmorning. Later he would have to get a shave. Well, not have to—but he should. They were having a Merchant's Association meeting later today, and he hadn't gotten a shave in four days. He had a light beard but after four days the stubble looked like dirt, and he thought—what the hell, though he didn't like the Association members—especially Hardesty, the banker who was one of those men who thought money gave them special privileges—they paid his wages. Might as well get a shave.

"Cell's clean," Clyde said as he came out of the back. He had his cup and he poured coffee from the cold pot on the stove, drank a cup down, gagged, then poured and drank another. "Don't you ever heat this swill?"

Murphy smiled. He liked Clyde. He was an easy drunk to handle. "Sorry it isn't up to your standards."

"Did I do anything wrong this time?"

"I don't know, did you?"

"Come on, Murphy. Tell me straight."

"Just the usual. Listen, Clyde, why don't you quit it? It's killing you."

"I know." Clyde looked out the window, then back at Murphy, down at the floor, and out again. "Maybe some of us are supposed to die. Maybe that's the way it works."

"That's bull and you know it. Liquor talking."

"Yeah. I know. I'll see you next time." Clyde walked out without looking back.

Murphy stood up, took his gun down from the peg in the corner, strapped it on, and settled the leather into place. It was a Smith .44 he had ordered from Jensen five years earlier. Heavy and tough, and if you used it for a club you didn't have to worry about it breaking. Not really accurate but it got the job done.

He turned to close the door leading back to the cells. No matter how clean they were kept, the smell from the buckets came toward the front, drifted out like a cloud if he didn't keep the door closed. While his back was turned the front door to his office slammed open so hard it bounced against the wall.

Murphy had been sheriff for nine years. The first year he was lucky to stay alive, stone lucky and knew it. It had been a boom time, the town was truly wild and several times he had been shot at and missed. Twice he was shot at and hit. Felt the numbing jerk of a bullet striking him, the confusion as he went down with the slug. But after the first year he worked to learn. One of the things he learned was that any fast, violent motion usually meant that somebody was going to try to kill you or hurt you.

When the door slammed open he went into a crouch, whirled around with his gun half out of his holster before he realized the person in the doorway was Petey Wilms, who was nine years old. He was small and towheaded, wearing his brothers' hand-me-down clothes that were so large they had wrapped around him while he was running and now made him look as if he were standing sideways. His eyes were as big as pie plates.

"You got to come, Mr. Murphy! You got to come right now!"

"Take it easy, Petey. Tell me what's wrong."

"It's Sarah Penches! You got to come now!" He turned and ran out the door before Murphy could stop him.

Murphy stepped outside and looked up the street to where Petey was running. There was a small crowd at the livery stable, twelve or so men, and he moved in that direction at a trot. When he got to the door of the livery he shouldered his way through and stopped just inside. The interior was dark and he could see nothing. It took him a few seconds to get his eyes accustomed to being in the darkened barn, and even then he saw nothing. He felt the hair come up on his neck.

"In the back," Randy Jensen called. "Look in the back stall on the ground."

In a shaft of pale light from the open door Murphy saw a corner of calico and thought, Oh, no! as he moved to the back. Pushed into the corner of the rear stall was the body of a small girl. She had been strangled with a leather strap, which was still tied around her neck. Her skirt was pulled up and thrown next to her head, and her underwear had been ripped away. There was blood. He leaned over and pulled her skirt down and thought, they don't have to see that; nobody has to see that.

Her name is Sarah Penches, he thought, and she is twelve. No, her name *was* Sarah Penches. God.

"She's tore all to hell," somebody said from the door. "It's just awful. . . ."

"That's enough of that." Murphy turned on them. He realized with a start that he had his gun in his hand, and he put it back in his holster. The gun, always the gun. "Everybody get the hell out of here. No, wait. Does anybody know anything about this? Anything at all?"

Silence.

"I thought not. Who found the body?"

Again, silence. Then a man stepped forward. "I did. I come to look for work and couldn't find the livery man, so I started looking around. When I found it—her—I started to come for you, but then this kid come by and he saw her and ran for you. So I thought I'd better wait here."

"You thought right. What's your name?"

"Hodges. Milt Hodges."

"Why don't I know you?"

"I'm new here."

"Miner?"

"Not yet. But I'm looking."

"All right, Milt Hodges. You go to my office and have some coffee. I'll come when I can. I want to talk to you some more. The rest of you, leave. Oh, somebody stop and tell Doc Hensley to come over here right away. He'll be at Midge's having lunch. Tell him it's an emergency. And don't anybody go and tell Clariss or Charley Penches about Sarah. I'll take care of that, hear?"

The last he had to yell. Some were leaving. He hoped they heard him and took heed but he was afraid they wouldn't. This was the kind of thing people loved to talk about. It would break the Pencheses right down the middle, just break them in half.

He looked down at the girl. Her eyes were

14

bulged. He thought of cutting the leather strap from her throat but changed his mind. She was gone. It wouldn't help her and maybe Doc could figure something out if Murphy didn't change or move anything.

So Murphy stood and waited, looking down at the bent and broken figure in the corner of the stall. He thought that sixty-four dollars a month wasn't enough.

Not near enough.

CHAPTER 2

MURPHY MADE THEM all leave. Old Colonel—the old man who took care of the livery and was named for the tobacco he chewed, which always left a stain down his chin—wasn't around. Murphy asked everyone to leave. It was one of the hardest things he had ever done because he didn't want to be alone with the small body. It was too much, too much of an evil thing to be alone with, to stand alone with in a darkened barn. His mind wasn't working yet. He couldn't bring himself to stand and stare down at her.

Looking for evidence wouldn't bring her back. Nothing would bring her back—and that was the only thing that would make it all right. Even if he could catch the bastard who had done it, it wouldn't bring her back, wouldn't bring back the small girl who laughed and followed her mother down the street; wouldn't bring back the quick smile, or the hand holding the doll, or the time Murphy had seen her playing dress-up in her yard with the other girl.

The other girl.

He would have to make certain the other girls in town were safe. There, his brain was starting to work. He would have to spread the word to keep the other children safe. It was a step, the first thing to do. Protect the living.

He took off his hat and used the side of his thumb to wipe sweat off the leather band. The hat was getting floppy, he thought, have to send it away and get it reblocked. Damn. Little Sarah was lying in the dirt and he was thinking of getting his goddamn hat blocked.

"Where is she?" Doc Hensley came running in from the light of the street and was stopped by the darkness. "Where is she?" He was a short man, fat-to-round and balding. He'd been a surgeon in the Civil War, when he was very young. When the war was done he could not be a quiet civilian doctor again. So much had hit him that he could not be still. He went west and worked the mining towns, dealing with the violent trauma that went hand in hand with taking gold from rock; blown off limbs, crushed legs and arms, and splattered fractures that reminded him of the war. Now getting old, he was going down with the town, content to live out his life. He had run from Midge's place without his coat, just grabbed his bag and ran. He wheezed now from carrying his own weight.

"Here. Up here, Dr. Hensley," Murphy said. Nobody called him "Doc" to his face, out of respect. He was good, very good, too good for the small town. "In the stall. But you didn't have to run. She's dead."

"I'll be the judge on that."

"Of course."

The doctor knelt next to the body, took a scalpel, cut the leather strap around her neck, and used a stethoscope to listen to her chest and the side of her neck. His hands felt her cheeks, her neck. Gentle hands, hands that had set her ankle when she broke it falling off a swing, hands that had wrapped a plaster cast around the ankle. Now he leaned back in the straw and dust and horse manure and said, "Gone. You're right. She's dead. Sweet little thing. I treated her when she had measles, then later when she cut her hand helping her mother kill chickens. Sewed her up and she didn't cry or make a sound— ahh, hell!, this is awful."

He put the stethoscope back in his bag, closed it carefully, snapped the brass latch, and stood. "Any idea on who did it?"

Murphy shook his head, then realized that the doctor wasn't looking at him. "No. I was hoping you could help me on that."

"Me? What in hell do I know about it? If I knew who did it, I'd kill the son-of-a-bitch, slow."

"I thought maybe you could examine her and see

if you couldn't tell me something about how it happened, exactly what happened and when. Maybe there's something we can learn that way." Murphy kept up a steady pressure. "I'm in a corner on this and can use all the help I can get."

The doctor shook his head. "I can try, but there's not much to learn. I can tell right now she's been dead over three hours and that she's been raped and strangled. That's about all there is to tell from the body. Except—well, maybe. . . . Yes, I'll give it a try. Help carry her to my office and I'll see what I can do."

Hensley had been on the edge of saying something else but Murphy knew when to leave it alone and he backed off. They took a door off a stall— lifted it off the hinges—and rolled the body onto it and covered it with a horse blanket. The doctor put his bag on it, and they lifted it—lighter than Murphy had expected but then Sarah had been small, was small—and carried her to Hensley's office. He had a tiny frame building at the same end of town as the livery, so at least they didn't have to go through town with it. But there were still some people watching, standing where they stopped, as Murphy and the doctor made their way across the street.

In the office Hensley pulled the body off the stall door onto the examining table and waved Murphy out. "I'll tell you what I find."

Murphy held back, wondering how to ask the next question. Cincherville did not have an undertaker. Normally that didn't matter. Bud Peterson, a carpenter, made a good pine coffin. The family took care of the rest and got the preacher. Undertakers were a waste of time. But in this instance . . .

"Well," Hensley asked. "Is there something else?"

Murphy nodded. "I need a favor, Dr. Hensley. I've got to tell the Pencheses about this and they're going to want to see her. It's going to be bad, real bad—bad as anything there is. But with Sarah looking the way she does it will be worse for them. I was wondering if you could, you know, make her look a little better." Murphy sighed. "I know it ain't what you do, but in this case . . ."

Hensley hesitated, started to say something, then nodded. "I'll do what I can. But give me some time. I'll want to examine the body, and then it will take some more time to . . . to clean her up. Give me a couple of hours."

"Thanks. I owe you for this."

"No. You don't owe me anything. Like I said, I treated her for measles. You don't owe me a thing."

Murphy went back into the street and crossed once more to the livery. There were still no people. He was glad because he wanted to be alone. When Sarah's body had been there it was hard to see anything else. He wanted to go over it once more and see if there was something he missed.

Inside the livery he stopped again to let his eyes get used to the darkness. When they did, he walked carefully to the rear and stood over where the body had lain. He did not know what he was looking for, or even if there was anything which might help him, but he stood and let his eyes go back and forth, working in little squares as if he were looking for something lost on the ground; on the fourth scan he saw some small dig marks. They might have been anything, but the angle and the shape made him think they could belong to the man who did this—pushing with his toes when he was on her. Murphy knelt and studied the marks more closely. On the right one, which would have been the right toe, there was a line as if there might have been a cut or notch out of the toe of the boot.

It probably meant nothing, but he filed it. Outside of the scuff marks, there was nothing to see in the immediate area. He started to work out and around, moving in larger and larger circles. There was still nothing. He was just about to give it up when he heard the scream.

It was a high-pitched, keening scream; a loud, cutting scream that went through him into his soul. He'd heard one like it before when he came across an Indian woman sitting next to her dead man. A cut scream.

He ran from the livery, his gun in his hand, thumb on the hammer. At the light of the door opening, he instinctively held to the side and went along the wall until the flash of the light had settled in his eyes. Then he looked down the street to where the scream was coming from and put his gun back in the holster.

Clariss Penches was running, staggering up the middle of the street. The sound came from her and he moved to intercept her, thinking he'd like to get the son-of-a-bitch who had told her. Some people just couldn't leave it alone. One of them had rushed to tell her, rushed to see it tear her. It was the one thing he'd learned more solid than anything else in nine years—people are mean. Given the chance, they're really mean down in their hearts.

"Clariss, hold it here." Murphy reached her and held out his arms, but she tried to duck around him. There were dusty smudges on her dress at the knees where she must have fallen in the street trying to run. She would never have dirt on her dress, he thought—not ever. She was a thin woman, with even brown hair and amazing strength. He caught her shoulder and she slipped away. He caught her wrist and held her. "Wait now, Clariss. Hold it here for a minute."

"Damn you, Al, don't you tell me to hold it. Is it true? Is my Sarah de . . . de . . . gone?" Her eyes were wild, animal eyes, filled with a savage grief so that he couldn't stand to look in them. Nobody could have, he thought. It was not a place any man could look without having his soul torn to pieces.

"Yes, Clariss. It's true. Now you hold it here for a time, please. Please. I'm sorry for it, but you hold it here."

"Where is she? You tell me where she is now, damn you, right now."

"At Dr. Hensley's. He's . . . she's at his place. Clariss, where is Charley? Can't we get Charley?"

"He's out to the McCormick hole setting up some shots. Now do you let me go or do I have to scratch your eyes out? I will, Al Murphy—I'll tear you."

"I'll go with you, Clariss." And it is the last thing I want to do, he thought, holding her arm and walking next to her toward Hensley's small house. After that I'll go to McCormick's and talk to Charley and that is the second-to-the-last-thing I want to do in my whole life.

CHAPTER 3

THERE WERE NO really decent mines left around Cincherville. For all of that, Murphy thought, riding out of town, there never had been any really decent mines. There were several small hits that had looked good, and there were some steady veins that paid off just enough to keep working them—mostly silver. A little gold.

But there had never been the wild strikes like up around Central City or Cripple Creek. It had boomed some. Cincherville was in the foothills and there had been some paydirt—it had boomed some, but never like the wild towns up in the mountains. Once a man had come through with a wagon load of strawberries, must have been seven or eight years ago, when they were still taking some metal. He had tried to sell them for five dollars a box. People had just laughed at him. When he objected and said he had sold berries for that up in Leadville during the boom, they laughed all the harder. Cincherville just didn't have that kind of a strike. Old Colonel had told the man with the strawberries that it was about a dollar-a-box boom and if he wanted a five-dollar-a-box boom town, he'd have to take them further up in the mountains.

Yet there were a couple of steady holes working. One of them was the McCormick mine, nine miles southwest of town up in a box canyon with sloping sides—more of a big wash than a canyon. A Scotchman named McCormick—nobody knew his first name—had hit a small amount of gold and a respectable amount of silver. They called it McCormick's hole even after he'd sold it and gone on, drinking whiskey from a green bottle until he puked. Some eastern corporation had bought it. They sent engineers out, and they kept plugging along, taking the hole down with the vein, year after year.

Mostly they hired local men to work it who usually did their own powder. But now and then they would hit a tricky shot, a ledge that had to be blown right, or a dump shot, and the men didn't feel they had the expertise. That's when they called in Charley Penches.

Charley had been an ordnance man in the army, had studied mining and rock-blowing up in Montana, before he came south, met Clariss, and got settled and married. When he was working in Montana he had run across a black man named Simpson Mann, who was the best powder man the mines had ever seen. They had some whiskey together and some talk. Charley wound up working with Simpson for almost two years. They said Simpson was so good he could use powder to blow the lid off a barrel of Du Pont's finest without setting off the powder inside. Probably not true, but Simpson had been really good. And that had rubbed off on Charley.

So when they had a tricky shot to set up, they called Charley in and paid him a fair consulting fee, which kept him going so he could work his own hole. It hadn't paid yet, but he thought it soon would. He was always talking about how he would take Clariss and Sarah back to Wisconsin when he hit and buy a small farm with black dirt and green, green grass and . . .

Sarah was gone, Murphy thought, watching the dust ahead on the two rut road. It was a wagon and he was catching up with it. He pulled his horse to the side, to ride out of the dust, but the horse was a hammer head Murphy had picked up four months earlier; the horse did what he wanted and slid back onto the road where the dust hung. Murphy resigned himself to getting dirty.

He shook his head at some flies that had followed the horse's sweat and thought they'd try his face. Come August and September they'd get worse, but they were already getting pretty bad.

How could he tell Charley?

The man had set the world on Sarah. How could he tell him? He thought back to the scene in Hensley's office when he took Clariss in. Hensley had the girl's body stripped on the table and hadn't been ready. He was doing something with a knife. Clariss had gone crazy—wild, frothing crazy at the mouth so that she didn't make sense. They both had had their hands full trying to hold her down.

Even when they got her settled, and Hensley got a sheet over the body, she wouldn't stop. She threw herself on the body and screamed and screamed, that same cutting scream she'd used coming down the street. Finally Hensley had gotten her to drink some kind of sedative, and they had put her down on the couch in the front.

How in hell could he tell Charley?

He was catching up to the wagon now. He heeled the ribs on the hammer head. The horse frogged a couple of times and came up into a jolting trot. Another nudge and the horse jerked into a hesitant gallop, still rough. Murphy came alongside the wagon and ahead of the dust. The cargo in the wagon was boxes of supplies, food, and barrels of flour, but he didn't know the man on the seat. Murphy nodded and signed the man that he wanted to talk a little. The driver slid over on the seat to get closer to Murphy but kept the team going.

"Hate to pull them down," the driver said. "They're finally working. If I stop them, they'll stiffen so bad I'll never get the bastards going again." He paused and spit juice over the side. He was younger than he looked—probably twenty five or six—but the dirt and the seams in his face made him look older than thirty. Pushing forty. "What can I do for you?"

"I'm the sheriff in Cincherville. On my way out to the McCormick hole and thought I'd have a few words. Don't believe I know you." He let it hang. Most times he learned more by not asking people what he wanted and letting them go on with it. Now and again they'd tell him more than he thought they knew. Just nudge them to get them started. Now and then he got more than he wanted to know.

"It's about that girl, isn't it?"

Murphy said nothing. He tried to see the man's boot toes but there was dirt on them, and he couldn't tell if the right one was scarred or not.

"I didn't have nothing to do with that."

Murphy nodded. "Didn't figure you did. Just wanted to know your name and how come I don't know you. Also, how'd you know about the girl?"

Another spit. The man appeared eager to please. Too eager? Murphy edged in the saddle so his gun was handier. He hated shooting off a horse. One of the times he'd been hit he'd been on a horse; he'd fired a shot and the damn horse had gone hog wild on him. While he was trying to stop it and get another shot off, the man he'd been shooting at used a rifle and put a .44-40 bullet through his right thigh. The bullet had gone on through and killed the horse—broke his back. Even though Murphy had been able to get a shot into the man's pump and put him down, he still hated shooting off a horse.

"You could of come right out and asked it like a gentleman."

"I'm asking."

Now the man was mad, but that was all right. Mad people said things they didn't mean to say, just like drunk people. But the man looked at Murphy's size and maybe at the badge; he backed down.

"Name is Wright. Clay Wright. I heard about the girl when I was going out of town. Some woman started screaming. I asked a rider going out ahead of me what was happening. I'm new in the McCormick hole. They brought me down from a hole up in Montana. I just been here a week. This was my first time in town—that's why you don't know me. And if you still think I had something to do with that little girl, maybe I'll stop this damn team and we'll get to dancing. You're big, but size ain't all of it, and I don't like people thinking what you're thinking."

Murphy shrugged. "I'm not thinking anything. And I didn't say you had anything to do with the girl. What about this rider who went out ahead of you? You know him?"

Wright settled a bit. There were flies working the rear end of his team, and he used the reins to brush them off—a sideways slide with the leather straps. A futile gesture, as they just resettled and started biting again. "I don't know who he was, but he wasn't in any big hurry. When I heard that woman scream—what *was* that? What was that woman screaming?"

"It was nothing. Tell me more about this man."

"I mean that scream cut like a knife. It was some awful . . ."

"It was the girl's mother. Now tell me about the man."

"Oh. I see. Well, that's too bad. Too bad. Damn." He was silent for a time, looking at the team ahead of him. "Not too much to tell about the man. He was on a big buckskin—biggest buckskin I ever saw. I asked him what was going on. He told me that a little girl had been attacked. I asked him about it, more questions, but he was close and tight. Then he rode off and I left. That's about it."

"What did he look like?"

"Kind of a thin guy, with a scar through one eyebrow."

That's Wilton Jamison, Murphy thought. Wil owned the beer parlor and had a cat girl upstairs, Fat Marge, who kept the miners happy when they got paid and came in from the holes. But Wil ran a reasonably straight place, a little poker, but the cards were all right. He kept the stakes down and threw the drunks out before they got mean. Why would he be leaving town in the morning? He never got up before noon. Slept in a room in back of the beer parlor and didn't come out until noon, if at all. "What did he say about the girl? How did he say it?"

"Just that a little girl had been attacked."

"Did he say it just like that? Attacked? Or did he say something else?"

Wright frowned, remembering. "No. Just that way—he just said a little girl had been attacked. That's all." With that he stopped and again watched his team. "I don't like talking about it. Not that way, you know what I mean? It's too ugly a thing to talk about."

Murphy nodded. "It's ugly, all right. Thank you, Clay Wright, for the help. I might want to talk to you again, if that's all right?"

"Anytime. I'm in the bunk shack out to the McCormick hole."

Murphy nodded and slammed his heels into the gelding. The horse snorted a bit and trotted, then finally broke into a jerky canter and pulled ahead of the wagon and team. Three more miles to the mine. Murphy knew there would be good water out there and some oats for his horse, so he piked his heels in again, wishing he'd worn spurs—he hated the way they clanked when he walked, made too much noise—and forced the horse into a faster gallop. The horse still didn't smooth and probably never would. Murphy would never be able to sell the damn thing, but he hated to admit he'd made a bad buy. He had two hundred in that horse and liked the size—sixteen hands—but Old Colonel had seen Murphy coming. And that was another thing. Where the hell was Old Colonel? Nobody had seen him. While he might be gone a day now and then, it was unusual. And this was not a good time for the old man to do unusual things, what with the body being found in his livery.

How in hell would he tell Charley Penches?

CHAPTER 4

THE McCORMICK HOLE was typical of the mines. Shacks scattered around a hole in the ground. They had a crusher shed built up on top of a tailing pile, all of gray wood, weathered and pitted, and four other shacks for the miners to sleep in and store tools, equipment, blasting powder, and dynamite. When Murphy rode into the mine area they were getting ready for a shot, and all the miners had been pulled out of the hole. A man with a red rag waved Murphy to stop, and he pulled the gelding up and got off. Usually when they shot there was little or no disturbance above ground—a mild thumping to the dirt. But if they were pulling the miners out of the hole it must be a tricky shot, perhaps a shallow one, and he didn't trust the gelding to hold for a loud noise. He pulled his pants

33

out of his crotch, stretched his legs, and walked to the man with the flag.

"Bad shot?"

The man nodded. "We're going off to the side, just inside. She might plug the hole when she goes. We didn't want to catch anybody down below."

"Know where I can find Charley Penches?"

Another nod. "In the hole, likely. It's his shot. But he should be right out. They must be close to firing."

As if on cue, Charley Penches came running out of the mouth of the mine—just over a hundred yards from Murphy—and trotted off to the side of the opening to get away from any debris that might blow out.

"Fire in the hole!" Charley yelled, first left and then right. Then he walked still further, saw Murphy standing with his horse and waved. Murphy waved back and handed the reins of the gelding to the flag man. "Hold this bastard, will you? I got to talk to Charley."

"Sure."

When Murphy was halfway to where Charley was standing there was a small thump in the ground. A ten-foot squirt of dust came out of the opening. That was it. Murphy turned and saw that the gelding hadn't moved—that was something, at any rate—and he walked up to Charley.

"Have to talk to you, Charley."

"You do?"

"Alone." He took Charley by the arm and

walked away from the other miners, who were moving slowly back to the hole. When they were beyond earshot of the others he put his body to block them from seeing Charley, and he told him, straight and simple and ugly and short, what had happened to the daughter who had meant the world to him. Murphy watched Charley's seamed face—not believe, believe, know, understand, then break and shatter. He started to go down, silently, as if hit with a hammer. Murphy caught him. "You got a horse or wagon out here?"

"Just a horse. He's in the stock pen over with the mules. Oh, god, how can this be—what about Clariss? Is Clariss all right?"

"Doc Hensley gave her something. She's sleeping."

Another try. He couldn't take it in yet. "Are you sure? Are you really sure it's Sarah and not somebody else?"

Murphy nodded. "I'm sorry. The sorriest I've ever been. But I'm sure."

"But who, why? How can this be? Not Sarah!"

"Let's get your horse. I'll go back to town with you."

Murphy led him to the stock pen and got Charley's horse saddled—all the while Charley just stood, staring at the hills, staring at nothing. He stood in numb silence. When Murphy had Charley's horse saddled Charley threw his leg over the saddle and was gone, raking the horse with bare bootheels, flogging the horse with his hat.

Murphy walked back to the flag man, got his gelding, ignoring the questions, and climbed on. He could not keep up with Charley without killing the gelding, or himself, but he nudged the horse—still without feed or water—into a light canter and headed back for town. Charley would likely ride the horse to death, or take it down to where it might as well be dead. Murphy wouldn't copy him.

A mile on the way back in he met the wagon he'd passed on the way out. The rest of the way into town he was alone. When he got to Cincherville he saw Charley's horse tied at Hensley's place. It was blown, sweat covered, and ready to drop. Murphy turned his gelding, untied Charley's horse from the rail, and took it to the livery with him. He hated to take a horse down like that, beyond where it could come back up. By rights the thing should be shot. There were flecks of blood on the horse's nostrils, and he stood with his legs spread to the sides. But Murphy led him to the livery.

Once there, he rode into the barn, leading Charley's horse—and dismounted. Still Old Colonel was nowhere to be seen, so he unsaddled and put Charley's horse in the back stall, opposite where Sarah had been found. He used a burlap sack to rub the horse down, found him some oats, and let him drink from the water tank before letting him out in the back corral. The horse would probably live if he didn't get lung problems but he would never be good again. Murphy spent ten more minutes working on his gelding, rubbing him down, graining and watering him, and then turned him out in back as well. The horse had given him somewhere over twelve miles and didn't look near tired out yet. He was starting to feel better about the two hundred dollars.

He put his saddle on his rented peg in the tack room at the end of the barn and walked back down the street toward his office. Charley and Clariss would want to be alone with Hensley for a time. They surely didn't need Murphy digging around, asking questions, until things settled a bit for them. If they ever did settle down again. It was coming onto evening. He hadn't eaten since morning breakfast at Midge's. He was on the edge of hunger but felt guilty about it, about being hungry after what had happened to Sarah. He'd settle for a sandwich later and a chance to talk to Midge. He sometimes felt the need to talk to Midge when things got down a bit, like now. It seemed to be happening more frequently. He wasn't sure if that was a good thing or a bad thing, but this night for sure he would like to see her. And talk to her.

For now, he would settle for a cold cup of coffee in his office. He kicked the dust off his boots, opened the door, and walked in.

"About time," said the miner, Milt Hodges. He stood up. "I waited two hours, then went off and had some lunch, then was going to keep going but I stopped and talked to some people. They said if

Murphy said to wait, I should wait. You got some people who believe in you, don't you?"

"Damn. I'm sorry. I clean forgot I sent you here to wait. I must be getting old."

Milt stretched. "Ahh, hell, I guess it don't make no nevermind. If push comes to shove, I don't have a hell of a lot to do anyway, except slow-starve."

"How about some coffee?"

"I'm way ahead of you. I drank what you had and made a new pot, though I liked to burn myself out of here when I fired the stove. It's too hot for anything but a kitchen stove. How about you, have some coffee? It's tough but good. I found some grind in your desk."

"Made yourself to home, did you?" Murphy looked at him, tried to bridle and get mad, but found himself liking the man instead. Milt was young, but seemed to have a brain for all that and a quick thought and smile. On the spur of the moment Murphy asked, "You pretty much down on your luck?"

"I don't know. I never been up on it long enough to know what down is like. Why you asking?"

"Maybe so I could use a little help. I can't pay much, just food, a bed, and some beer money. But I need somebody to give me a hand, and you might be the one."

"You're hiring the man who found that girl's body to be a deputy?" Milt shook his head. "How do you know I ain't the one you're looking for?"

"I don't. But I don't think you would have

waited if you were. And if I find you are the one, you'll just be closer. Handier."

"Well, I ain't. And I'll take the work, at least until something else comes up. What do you want me to do?"

"First, tell me what you can remember about when you found her. Then we'll go to Midge's and get some food. Then I'll start you on rounds." He noticed that Milt wasn't wearing a weapon. "You got a gun somewhere?"

"Nope. Had a rifle but I swapped it for some food awhile back." Milt smiled. "I noticed you had a Colt in your desk. I could take that if you want me to. But I can't hit a bull's ass at four feet with one of the damn things."

"Carry it, anyway. Later, when you go on rounds, just stick it in your belt. There's a box of shells in the same drawer."

"I saw them."

Murphy took some coffee and sipped it. Strong, almost too strong, but with that good edge of almost chocolate flavor he liked. Maybe he could get the board to approve hiring a deputy full time. He sat in back of his desk. "So tell me everything you can about how it was when you found her. Every little thing."

Milt took his cup and went to the bench by the window. He sat slowly, thinking. "I honestly don't think there's much to tell that you don't know already. I came in the barn looking for the man who runs the livery—what's his name?"

"Old Colonel."

"I came in looking for him and there she was, lying there."

"What did you want Old Colonel for?"

"I thought maybe I could clean the barn and make enough for a meal or some bacon and flour. Damned prices are crazy. A dollar for five pounds of flour. Who ever heard of such a thing?"

Murphy nodded. "I know. But what else, think now."

"Nothing. She was down, in the dirt and straw, and when I ran out to find you—or find the law, I mean—that little kid ran in and saw her. He passed me by a mile, heading for your office. So I stayed."

"Nobody else?"

"You mean in the barn? No. Leastways none I could see. And I didn't hear anything, either. Then some other people came—I don't know any of them—and stood there, gawking. Then you came."

Murphy was silent for a time, thinking. He finished his coffee and stood. "Well. That's it for now. Let's go get something to eat at Midge's."

"I hope she's got a lot," Milt said, following him out the door. "I'm going on three days without a sitdown meal."

"I probably made a bad move putting you on. I'll go broke just feeding you."

CHAPTER 5

Midge's Cafe had formerly been a slop chute to feed miners. A man named Porter had owned it and called it the Bonanza. Figuring on a bigger boom than Cincherville had, he had put in wooden plank tables and benches, and a cookstove in the back room. He nailed metal plates to the table and sold stew by the dipperful for two dollars. But as with the man with the strawberries, Porter ran smack into the Cincherville small-boom principle, took freight, and pulled out one Saturday. About four months later Midge's husband—a thirty-seven-year-old dreamer named Hans—had been killed in a rock drop in the McCormick hole, and Midge found herself on the short end of living.

Ladies in mining towns were limited to few occupations to make a living. They could sell

41

themselves, or do laundry, or cook. Midge was high on pride, so that took out the first; since she hated laundry, that put her in line to move into the old Bonanza and set up a business. She cooked meat and potatoes and bread and put out a good plate for a dollar—high priced, but not crazy high. She cleaned the plates, tried to get fresh milk when she could, and used clean flour for the bread. For a time miners came to call, some with honorable intentions, some not, but she didn't think much of any of them and gradually, over the three years she'd been in Cincherville, Midge came to be left alone. She was a plain woman, but strongly built and holding a clean beauty that wasn't pretty so much as honest. She and Murphy had a settled feeling between them, a talking feeling. Twice it had gone beyond talk but then had dropped back to where it was now—a knowledge between them. It was understood that they were friends, and that it would someday be more, but that was all for now. Murphy wasn't keen on the idea of dragging a woman into a marriage with a sheriff and Midge was her own woman.

So they talked. The weathered sign over the door still said Bonanza, but everybody called it Midge's cafe. Murphy liked going there. It was, in truth, the only place left in Cincherville that Murphy liked going to. He knew that it was pulling him down a road to something but he didn't much care. If it came to be, so be it. A man could do much worse than Midge, and he was getting close to the end of sheriffing, anyway.

He stepped through the door first and hung his hat on a peg to the right; Milt followed him in. It was still a bit early for supper, so there were only four others eating—all miners he knew.

Midge came out of the kitchen when she heard the door, saw Murphy, and smiled. "Look who's here. You want some coffee?"

Murphy nodded. "Two of them. This is Milt Hodges, my new helper. He'll need some coffee and lots of food."

The two men took a table in the corner, Murphy sitting with his back to the wall and facing the door. Those things were automatic—sit facing a door, always stop far enough from somebody so they can't hit you, always get the sun at your back, always watch hands. He didn't even think of those things anymore. Midge brought two cups of coffee and smiled lightly at Milt. "I'll get you some plates soon. The gravy has to simmer a bit."

"Biscuits or bread?" Murphy asked.

"Biscuits. My yeast soured off too much."

To hell with a sandwich, Murphy thought. He had to eat. And Midge's biscuits were fine, just fine. "That's good."

She held back for a moment—normally she didn't talk about his work. He didn't like to discuss it, but he could see something eating at her, so he asked, "What's wrong?"

She frowned. "Well. I don't really want to talk about it, but it's bothering me some."

"Sarah."

She nodded. Some hair had come loose from her pull-back and she tucked it in back of her ear. Full and brown, the hair tended to look curly in the evenings when the humidity rose. "Is all that true—what I've been hearing?"

"I don't know what you've been hearing."

"That she was, you know . . . used."

He nodded. The other miners in the room were silent, looking at him. He shot them a mind-your-own business look. "It's not something you want to talk about."

"No. Except that, well, come into the kitchen." She turned suddenly and went back through the kitchen door. He rose to follow. Milt started up but Murphy signed him down. "Drink your coffee."

In the kitchen Midge passed the stove and stood by the pump, back in the corner. He leaned down and she spoke softly in his ear. "It's probably nothing, but there were some men in here talking yesterday. They were a little drunk. Not bad, just talking a little too loud. Anyway, one of them saw Sarah walk by the window outside and said how it wouldn't be long before she would be ready for business."

"Who was it?"

"I can't be sure because I was in the kitchen. I didn't see which one said it; there were four men at the table. But I think it was Randy Jensen. The other three were miners, but I don't know them. They come in, but not very often."

Murphy nodded. Randy Jensen owned the dry-goods store and once of a week he took a drink. He was single, having lost a wife in birthing—wife and stillborn baby—and he was also one of those who had made some early attempts on Midge. But he didn't make trouble, or hadn't, and it didn't figure that Randy had done that to Sarah. On the other hand, it didn't figure that anybody had done that to Sarah.

"What did he say—exactly?"

"Just that. 'There goes that Sarah Penches. She looks like it won't be long before she's ready for business.' Then I came out and they quit talking about it."

He nodded. "Well. It probably means nothing, like you say. Just keep it to yourself."

"Sure. But if that little son-of-a-bitch did it, I don't want him here anymore."

Murphy started. He had never heard her use strong language before, had never seen her fire up. "I understand. But he's probably not the one." Murphy had no idea why he said that, or felt that. "We'll watch him. Don't worry." He could see that she was still upset. He wanted to say more to comfort her, but the front door of the cafe slammed open and a man's voice yelled.

"Looking for Murphy! Anybody seen him?"

Murphy stepped out from the kitchen. "I'm here. What's the matter?"

"Come to the livery. Somebody just found Old Colonel all cut to hell like a hog."

Oh, no, he thought. Another one. "On the way." He saw that Milt was already on his feet, had his hat on, and was waiting by the door; Murphy hadn't seen him move at all. Just as smooth as silk.

Murphy grabbed his hat and ran for the door.

Down the street at the livery he saw another crowd gathered—fifteen or twenty people this time. A couple of kids. They weren't going in and they parted to let Murphy and Milt trot past.

There was nobody in the barn. The light was failing outside. It made their eyes feel better inside, but they couldn't see anybody until a voice cried, "Up here. I'm up in the loft."

"Stay down," Murphy told Hodges. "I might want you down here."

The deputy nodded and Murphy went to the loft ladder. "Who's up there?"

"Bill Tison. I come up here looking for hay to throw down and found him in the back of the loft. I already sent for the doctor."

I should have searched the whole barn, Murphy thought. Stupid. I should have gone over the whole thing right this morning. He went up the ladder without pulling his gun. Bill Tison was the telegraph operator-lineman-message receiver for Western Union. A young man with a cowlick and wide eyes.

"Over here. He's back in the corner. I rode out to check that line near Johnson's wash. It was leaning pretty bad, and I thought I might prop it up a bit. When I got back Old Colonel wasn't anywhere around. So I thought I'd throw hay down myself. And that's when I found him."

What a day, Murphy thought, going back to the body in the rapidly darkening loft. What a goddamn day this is.

Old Colonel was sprawled in the hay on his back, his throat cut, and blood splattered all across the hay and his clothes. His face was in a rigid grimace. His hands were still clutched at his abdomen where there were three puncture wounds across, just above his belt. His shirt had been pushed up and the wounds looked strangely familiar to Murphy. Not bullets, but something about the spacing . . .

"I figure somebody shoved a hayfork in his belly. Then cut his throat. That's how it looks to me." Tison was leaning down next to Murphy, squinting in the dark. "Want I should go get a lantern?"

Another expert, Murphy thought. But he was right. "Yes. Get a lantern. But get a closed one. This hay is dry as tinder."

The request was needless. Milt was already coming up the ladder with a closed kerosene lantern, throwing a yellow glare. "Found it by the tack room. Figured you might need it. What is it? . . . Jeesus!"

"Thanks for the lantern. Go back down and bring the doctor up here when he comes. I'll want his opinion before I move the body."

Milt went back down the ladder. Bill Tison stood

up. "So, what do you figure? He saw what happened to Sarah and somebody killed him to keep him quiet? Is that what you figure?"

Suddenly, tightly, hotly, Murphy was angry. Not at the kid, mad at the bastard who thought he could run around Murphy's town killing people. But the anger came out on Tison. "Billy, I don't figure anything yet. Now why don't you just take your scrawny little ass back down the ladder and leave me alone to do my job?"

"Yes, sir. Yes, sir. I didn't mean to get you all high and mighty like this—pardon me for living." He went down the ladder and Murphy went back to the body.

Old Colonel had been ugly in life. In death he was grotesque, hideous. His mouth gaped open in the amber glow from the lamp, his teeth dark with tobacco stains, his eyes wide and sightless. Murphy looked around in the hay but could see nothing. They would search thoroughly this time, all around the loft and barn.

He was through making stupid mistakes.

CHAPTER 6

MILT CLEARED THE barn smoothly, without making anybody mad, which was better than Murphy would have done had he gone down in his anger. He would have started throwing people.

Done and done, he thought, I am done being a horse's ass on this one. He hung the lantern on a nail, high to scatter light all around the haymow, although it left the area still dusky, then began his search. He started out at the wall, went completely around the hayloft on his hands and knees, inch by inch. When he was nearly done with the first circuit he found the fork.

Three tines of spring steel and a hickory handle. It had been thrown over to the side. There was dried blood on the tines. That might mean something, he thought—the blood is dried. Hell, I'm grabbing at straws. It means the blood is dried, that's what it means.

"How things going up there?" Milt called up the ladder. "Need help?"

"No. Just keep the people away and send Doc up when he comes."

"You got it." Milt turned from the loft and went back to the door.

Murphy studied the pitchfork closely, not sure what he was looking for, letting his eyes work for his mind. He had a sudden, intense mental picture of Old Colonel in the loft forking hay and the pitchfork being driven into his soft whiskey belly.

No. That didn't work. Something about the setup didn't work. Old Colonel would have been up in the loft getting hay to throw down to his rental horses. He heard something—wait. When? That's first. When? Not the night before, because Sarah would have been missing all that night. And that would have been noticed. So it hadn't happened yesterday. Yesterday, he thought, there was still a Sarah and Old Colonel. No, Murphy had to stop that—thinking like that—and concentrate on finding the killer.

He pulled his turnip watch out of his vest pocket and saw that it was almost six. All day gone now, one day—was that all? One day? The ticking from the watch filled the whole loft, made him suddenly feel spooky. He put it back. It was six and would be dark soon. That's why the light was so bad. And it all pointed to Sarah having been . . . attacked this morning.

So start again, he thought. This morning, early, Old Colonel is in the loft throwing hay down for morning feed on the rentals and he hears something downstairs.

And whoever is attacking Sarah, or has attacked Sarah—Murphy's thoughts finished lamely—comes up the stairs, takes the pitchfork away from Old Colonel and stabs him with it.

Hell, that's not even close. It just doesn't work. Even though Old Colonel was getting on in years, fat and too fond of whiskey, it would take a hell of a man to wrestle the fork away from him—if Old Colonel *was* standing at the top of the ladder holding the fork. There would have been a fight, a yell. Somebody in town would have heard something. Hell, you could pee from one side of this town to the other; somebody would have heard the fight.

"What in hell is going on?" Doc Hensley stuck his head up through the loft entry. "Somebody said you had Old Colonel up here . . . " He trailed off as he saw the body.

Murphy was standing to the side holding the pitchfork. "Yeah. He's dead—and I don't need to have you confirm it. He's dead twice. Stuck and slashed."

Doc rubbed his face, exhaustion making the lines deeper. "I left both Pencheses at my office with the body. They're going to take care of her. I said that I would do it because I wanted to make it nicer, you know, but when I saw the look in Charley's eyes I shut up. He's terrible with rage. You might have to watch him." He stood over Old Colonel. Some barn flies had followed the blood smell up from the manure and were settling on the wounds to plant maggot eggs. "And now this. . . ."

The lantern flickered and flared as it started to use up the last of the kerosene. Murphy went to the ladder to call down to Milt. "Run over to the office and bring that other closed lantern, will you? And that small half-gallon can of lamp oil. We'll be up here a time."

"You got it," Milt said and was gone. Murphy wondered, fleetingly, how long it would take him to get sick of Milt saying "You got it." Maybe one more time. He turned back to Doc. "Same as before—if you can figure out about when it happened it would help a lot. And the same on other things. Anything you can find."

Doc waved flies away from the throat wound. "Sharp knife. It's a clean cut. Clean and deep. Even cut the esophagus, and that takes a bit. Doesn't look like it was done with a sawing motion, so it must have been sharp and quick." He stood and looked down, measuring with his eyes. "See here, now."

Murphy put the fork down. "See what?"

"The cut is off at a bit of an angle. It's not

straight across. If you stand and look down square you can tell it."

Murphy looked at Old Colonel and after a bit nodded. "I see. But I'm not sure what it means."

Doc shook his head. "It might mean nothing. If he was cut from the front it doesn't mean a thing. But if he was cut from the rear, cut across and let to drop over and down on his back, it might mean the killer was left-handed. Of course, it might not, too. I saw a lot of cuts in the war—damned sabers. The angle there was more pronounced, hacking down from the left or right. But it's the same. The cutting, even with a sharp knife, would make whoever was doing it pull down at that angle to cut deep. So it might mean he was left-handed."

"Or not. If he was cut from the front . . ."

"It's something."

"It's something." Murphy nodded. "And I need anything and everything."

"Is that the fork he was stuck with?"

"Yeah. Looks like it."

Doc picked it up, looked at it, shook his head. "Too bad. I thought there might be fingerprints in the blood but there aren't any."

"Fingerprints? Are you serious?"

"I'm always serious. I read an article in one of those journals that was about some research on fingerprints. They say the lines—they call them loops—are different for everybody, and that it might be a way to identify an individual accurately.

I thought if there were prints in the blood, we might somehow be able to use them."

Hell, Murphy thought—and I figured I was coming off the wall with things like dried blood. Doc must be really hit by this with Sarah.

Milt came into the loft with the lantern, already lighted, and the can of oil. He wrinkled his nose. "Smells like a slaughterhouse up here.

"Who is this?" Doc asked.

"Milt. My new helper."

But Doc was back at the body, mumbling as he worked. "Can't tell how long. The body has rigor, but that lasts for hours, depending on the heat and air. It's a good guess that he's been dead all day, though."

"About the same as Sarah."

"Well, hell, wouldn't you say that?"

Murphy nodded. "Of course. I'm just trying to get this worked out. Some parts of it don't make sense."

Doc looked up from the body. "None of it makes sense. The thing with Sarah—I had time for a detailed examination. She was done twice—both ways. And it was while she was alive. The son-of-a-bitch did it while she was still alive. She knew it was happening."

The three men were silent for a time, each lost in his thoughts, standing in the flickering yellow light from the lanterns in the loft, the body sprawled out before them.

Finally Milt broke the silence. "I saw a picture of

a prospector they found up in the Black Hills a few years back. It was tacked to the side of an assay office as a warning. The Sioux had caught him. There must have been forty, fifty arrows in him. Looked like a porcupine. Then they'd gutted him and cut his dingus off and shoved it in his mouth." Murphy and Doc looked at him. "I was just wondering if, when we catch this bastard, we could get those Sioux down here for a day or two."

Doc grunted but said nothing and turned back to the body. When he had finished examining the wounds and had found nothing further, he had Milt help him turn the Old Colonel over. Doc looked for injuries on the back, but there was nothing. When he had finished he put the magnifying glass he'd been using in his bag, closed it with the small belt wrapped around it, and stood. "You get somebody to help get him down and over to my office. He didn't have any family that I know of. And not too many people who did horses with him were friendly with him. So I'll get a box and a preacher, and we'll bury him. But I'll be damned if I'm going to get him down."

Doc left. Murphy decided against calling for help, since he had not finished the barn yet and didn't want people tracking around. So Milt and Murphy took the Old Colonel down themselves. In the end, due to his bulk and size, they had to lower him with a rope like he was so much meat. Then they took another stall door and carried him over to Doc's, across the road.

At one point Milt's legs sagged and he stumbled. "Heavy, isn't he?"

"He could eat," Murphy said.

"Speaking of that, I never did get anything to eat at the cafe."

"You can think of food now?"

"I'm about to cave in."

"Midge is closed for the night," Murphy replied.

"I kind of got the idea when we were over there before that she might not mind opening late for you."

Murphy looked at him. There had been a time when, if Murphy looked that way, men began to feel small. "Just what is that supposed to mean?"

Milt shook his head. "Nothing . . . nothing like that. It's just the way she looked at you, and the way you talked to her. I thought there was something between you, that's all."

"Not to talk about."

"Sorry. Nothing meant by it."

Murphy was about to say more but they got to Doc's about then and had to horse the body up the steps and into the office. The lights were on and Doc sat with a cup of amber liquor in his hand. "Charley and Clariss must have taken Sarah home, so just put him on the steel table in the back.

When they were done Murphy took Milt over to the cafe and knocked on the door. The main lights were blown out, but through the window they could see Midge's hand lantern in the back. They watched the glow move as she came to the front and opened the door for them.

"I hate to bother you, Midge, but he claims he's dying of hunger."

She had a wrap around her shoulders and it set her hair off. A brown wrap to match her hair. Murphy turned his eyes away before his stare could mean more than he wanted it to mean.

"Come in," she said, moving back. "I figured you'd be back and kept a plate of stew and some biscuits and coffee for you."

They followed her into the back, the kitchen, where, as she said, there were two plates heaped with potatoes and stew. After washing at the hand pump, they sat to eat and were silent, until Milt had wiped up the last of the gravy with a piece of biscuit.

"That was some' fine," Milt said. "Just awful fine. I haven't been fed that fine since I was a boy at my grandma's."

Midge had been standing at the stove; she took the pot and refilled their cups. "It's easy to feed somebody who's starving."

"Well, I wasn't starving," Murphy said, "and I agree. That was the best stew I've had in years." He leaned back in the chair and lifted his gunbelt to ease the weight of the Smith. He took a sip of coffee and wondered how she knew to keep the stove kindled and warm, knew that they would be coming back to eat, knew so much about Murphy and what he was going to do. And she stood so straight and right—and her eyes were so deep brown . . .

"That's a funny look, Mr. Murphy," she said, smiling. "Are you thinking of crime?"

"Ahh . . . that. There *is* that. No, I wasn't, but I'd better start earning my pay pretty soon, hadn't I?"

"This is a terrible business, just a terrible business. Do you have any ideas yet?"

He shook his head. "No. No ideas at all. Keep your ears open, will you? And thanks for the supper."

He went outside and Milt followed, without saying anything except "thank you" to Midge. Murphy looked at his watch. "Coming on midnight. We'll check the saloon, then you get some sleep in the office. I'll wake you about three."

"What for?"

"Because I want somebody awake and watching this blasted town every minute until we get the son-of-a-bitch. I don't want any more bodies showing up."

"You got it."

Murphy winced in the darkness.

CHAPTER 7

THE SALOON WAS the same as all the saloons in all
the boom-and-die towns there were, Murphy
thought every time he came to check it out. It was a
board building, drafty with high ceilings, one card
table in back, and a billiard table so close to dead
the felt was almost gone. Wil had ordered felt to
replace it, he said, but it never had come, so they
shot billiards on the lumps. Down the right side as
he came in the door, which was not a batwing
because the weather was too cold in the winter,
Murphy saw the bar, little more than wood plank-
ing nailed to cross pieces with some spittoons
which the chewers almost always missed. No mir-
ror. Not in mining towns. Not for long, anyway.
Nothing fancy lasted long in mining towns. Two
pump lanterns hung from the cross members in the

board ceiling, one over the center of the room and one roughly over the card table. They hadn't been cleaned in months, so the light they cast had a white-yellow sheen that made it hard to see anything through the thick smoke.

And all over—the stink of drinking and smoking. Enough to gag a maggot on a gut wagon. Inside the door Murphy moved easily to the left and stood for a moment. Coming off a dark street into a lighted room, his eyes took a second or so to get used to the light. He didn't like to get deep into the room until he was ready. Another learned precaution, now automatic.

It was the usual crowd for midnight. Weekends the miners would come in from the McCormick hole and raise hell. But during the week there was a small crowd. Usually Wil closed early, about twelve-thirty during the week, but this night there were five men sitting at the table playing penny-ante poker. Wil was nowhere in sight. The bartender, a man named Al who everybody called Skeeter, was missing one hand—a mining accident years before—and had a wooden hook in its place. He was wiping the bar with a rag on his hook and nodded at Murphy when he came in with Milt, but said nothing.

Clyde was standing at the bar alone. Somewhere he had found a quarter or fifty cents—even Murphy did not know how he got money, but he always had enough for drinking—and he was getting efficiently, professionally, and completely drunk.

"Evening, Clyde," Murphy said. "Getting it done, I see."

But Clyde said nothing to him. He was a quiet drunk, sometimes surly but never mean. Still, when he was drinking, drinking was what he did. And he didn't like to talk about it. In the later stages he could get offensive. That's when Murphy would take him in. But this night Murphy knew Clyde would not get to that stage (Clyde usually was good for at least two nights following a night in jail) so Murphy didn't spend much time on him.

Murphy stepped to the bar and held up two fingers. "Beer, Skeeter, for both of us. And some talk."

Skeeter held two mugs in his good hand and worked the draft lever with his hook, slid the beers down the bar, and followed them. "Awful about today."

Murphy didn't say anything. He had heard enough about this day. He sipped the beer, saw Milt do the same. It was flat—the kegs never held the bubbles—and it was warm. But it cut the smoke a bit. "Where's the boss?"

"You mean Mr. Jamison?" Skeeter's voice had a slight sarcastic edge to it. "Mr. Jamison hasn't been in all day. Mr. Jamison left this morning for somewhere on a horse. I haven't seen him."

That fit in with what the skinner had said on the way out to the mine. "Didn't say where he was going?"

"Mr. Jamison don't tell me where he's going, you know that. I'm just the help."

The problem with Wil Jamison was that he was good looking, thought he was even better looking, and was always looking for a way to turn a dollar. He thought all the world of himself, thought he was God's gift to the ladies and as slick as a new calf. Just about everybody hated him. But it was a cordial hate and he ran a fair bar—stinking, but fair. He had hired Skeeter. Paid him twenty a month and all he could drink and steal, when nobody else in the world would take on a cripple. Skeeter shrugged. "Sorry I can't be more help."

Murphy turned to look at the game. Somebody won a hand. There was mild swearing and some throwing of cards, but all pretty settled. He knew all five players. Three were card bums, regulars who never really won or lost but just kept shuffling the money back and forth among themselves. Two of the others were miners from the McCormick hole, probably in town on a supply run and trying to stretch it overnight. One of the miners had won. There were two or three bills in the pot, so it must have been a fairly wild hand. But the tone eased down into the next hand. The winner of the last pot turned and ordered five nickel beers. And the game went on. And on.

"You going to close soon?" Murphy asked Skeeter.

Skeeter shook his head. "Mr. Jamison has a

rule—never close when somebody is on his feet and buying a beer."

"Even him?" Milt pointed with his chin at Clyde.

"Even Clyde," Skeeter said, nodding. "But he'll run out of nickels soon. The game might go all night."

"Keep them quiet," Murphy said, putting his beer down and heading for the door. "We got real people sleeping."

Skeeter nodded, but Murphy and Milt were gone.

In the street the sheriff moved away from the lighted door, off to the darkened side, and stood, waiting for his eyes to get used to the dark. It was the worst time, coming from a lighted building into a darkened street, and he hated it. He spoke in a lowered voice to Milt.

"This is where you'll have trouble. Coming out of a lighted room, your eyes aren't ready. This is the worst place if you're worried. This, and when two other people are fighting and you have to stop them. Like as not, nine times out of ten, they'll both turn on you."

Milt nodded but knew Murphy couldn't catch the nod in the dark, so he said aloud, "I'll remember that."

"All right. You work down the other side of the street, go back to the office, and get some sleep. I'll get you up at three or four. You can watch while I get some rest."

"I know this sounds dumb, but what are we looking for?"

"Nothing—same as always. It would be nice if we could catch him like this, but we probably won't. But with us out here, he might be kept from doing it again. That's what we're doing. And that's what about ninety percent of this job is all about. Standing around so you can be seen."

"Sounds about the same as being a target."

"Does, doesn't it?" And for the first time that day Murphy allowed himself a small smile. "I never thought of it that way—but that's the job. Go to sleep, I'll come for you in a bit."

Midnight to three.

He made his rounds—what they paid him for. When they gave Murphy the badge, the town manager—they didn't have a mayor—was a pompous man named George Smith. He was the banker then, but since had died of frozen heart (as they often said of him). Hardesty had moved up from being the cashier to owning the bank. But when Murphy had stepped forward, had volunteered for the sheriff's job, Smith had made a speech about citizens and peace and law and order. No, he had said something about ". . . law and good order."

And that's what they pay me for, Murphy thought. Maintaining law and good order. And the major part of that was making the rounds at night. During the day he handled town matters from his desk, sometimes dozing with his feet up. But at night he earned his keep. He went down the north side of the street first, checking the doors, the bank, the dry-goods store, and the machine shop where they did tooling for the miners now and again. When he had done the whole street, he went down in back of the buildings, checking the rear. Then he went across the street and did the same for the south side, checking Midge's, the saddle and harness store, and the feed store. Then the backs.

Nothing.

He kept circulating, moving with the shadows. Past the buildings on the north side of main street there was a row of houses, up a bit on a rise, above the dust and dirt of the street. Here the people who ran the stores, the bank, and the shops lived—away from their work. Above it. He made one round there, walking in plain view down the road, and tried to imagine which of them it was, if any.

The Merchant's Association. They were supposed to meet tonight. Murphy was supposed to have been there. But he guessed they had dropped it because of this business with Sarah. And he hadn't gotten his shave yet. And he didn't give a damn any longer.

Something like this, he thought, standing in the dark again, looking at the row of houses, something like this changed everything, changed the way you felt about people.

It might not have been anybody in town. It could

have been somebody passing through. But his feelings about all the men he knew had changed, had darkened.

He thought of the crime again, tried to make it work in his mind. How had Old Colonel been taken that way? Did the man see him, talk to him, and get the fork away somehow? But how could the man have managed to come up the ladder if Old Colonel knew about Sarah and was waiting at the top with a pitchfork?

It didn't fit.

Loud noises from the saloon. Some more swearing. He thought there might be a fight starting, but when he got to the door he saw he was wrong. The card game was breaking up and the two miners from the McCormick came out. They had horses tied to the rails, where they'd left them all night without loosening the cinches; when the men mounted, one of the horses objected with a couple of hops, but the men got settled and headed out of town. The three regulars stayed to have a beer with Skeeter, then came out and made their way to their rooms in different parts of the town. Skeeter blew the lamps out, locked up, and went into his room in the back of the saloon to sleep. It was a shed, really, Murphy thought, but not much different from his room.

He thought of his room, standing alone in the now completely darkened town. There was no moon. With no lights, it was so completely dark that it drove his thoughts inward. His room. Three steps by three steps, flat walls with no pictures, no paper, just bare, painted wood. A stand with a pitcher, a brass bed with a feather mattress, and a chamber pot underneath the bed. One standing closet with three shirts, three pants, and a hook for his gun.

A hook for his gun.

That was his home. His room. All he had to show. And with that thought came a softened image of Midge, of her room—he'd been there two times now, been there to spend time with her. It had pictures, gentle pictures, curtains—and frills and softness. He found himself thinking more and more of her room and of what she was coming to mean to him. He had to have more than a bare room with a hook for his gun. Maybe when this was done he would find some flowers and take them to Midge and . . .

Something stopped him. He took in half a breath, let it out, and moved his eyes back and forth. There had been movement. Something. He stepped back into the deep black between two buildings and watched, waiting. He eased the Smith out of his holster but held it in back of his leg so the metal wouldn't pick up some errant light. He waited, looking across the street.

There, again, a movement. Definite now. The dark shadow of a man, almost—just—a thickening in the night, moved away from the back of the saloon and started to the front. Murphy brought the gun up, aimed, waited. The figure was walking bent over, coming straight at him, and didn't seem to be sneaking. When the bent shadow was halfway across the street Murphy snorted and lowered the handgun.

Clyde.

Drunk, he probably had passed out in the back of the saloon. He was up now and moving, but most likely in a blackout. Murphy reholstered and stepped back out of sight. Clyde shuffled past, not three feet from Murphy, mumbling and swearing to himself. He had no idea Murphy was standing there. The old drunk would wander around and then fall asleep until midmorning on some sacking or in the dirt. He wouldn't cause any trouble. If Murphy took him in, there would be yelling, swearing, and puking in the cell. Easier to just leave him alone.

Murphy pulled out his watch and looked at the dial, saw it was after three, and went for Milt. Murphy would let the younger man work the rest of the night, while Murphy caught a little sleep. Maybe three hours. He was fogged with tiredness, fogged and down with it. And not coming up with any answers. Maybe a bit of rest would help. This damn business, he thought, walking to the office in the dark.

Just that. This damn business.

CHAPTER 8

MURPHY WAS NEVER sure if it was a dream. It was always the same.

There was a large fight at the saloon. Something about cards or drinking or Fat Marge in the upstairs crib room. The reason for the fight didn't matter, just that it was a fight, a big fight, and Wilton Jamison had sent Skeeter to the office to get him.

Murphy went running. When he got to the saloon there were men coming out through the windows and the door, fighting, swearing, and bellowing. Many of them, most of them, were laughing. That was the only thing not real about it. The men were all fighting and laughing. And Murphy thought that was wrong—that they shouldn't be laughing. In real, gut fights they didn't laugh; they were too busy trying to keep their eyes or throat intact to laugh. Now they were all laughing but he didn't let it stop him. He pulled his Smith and went wading in, slamming heads and jerking collars to separate them—and he started laughing. He couldn't help it. The laughter just came. As if there were some giant joke, some joke they all knew, something so secret that they couldn't even tell what the joke was, only that something was grandly, wonderfully funny. And it was always the same. Always the same.

At the height of the fight, when it was the worst and the funniest, when they were slamming, jerking, fighting, and laughing the most, he worked his way to the middle. He was in the center of the saloon with the card table tipped, blood flecked on the ceiling, and his hands wrapped in somebody's hair. While he got ready to pistol whip somebody, he looked up and saw the man.

The man stood in the back of the room and seemed so familiar, so close and familiar that Murphy's mind almost said hello—a silent hello to the figure in the shadows outside the fight.

Then he saw the gun.

The man was in the dark—partially. Murphy couldn't tell who he was, only that he knew him, knew him well, perhaps too well; the man's gun and arm stuck out into the light. Murphy could see them well. It was an old gun, a .45, a long Colt single action—an old thumbbuster with so much bullet it could damn near knock a horse over.

Oh, he thought. Just in that way. *Oh.* But he did not feel the menace of it, knew only the laughter, the wild joke of the moment, the joke of the fight.

Then the man's thumb pulled the hammer back and Murphy knew. Instantly, on cue, all the laughter stopped: the fight stopped. All the men backed away from him in serious piety. And he knew the joke, knew the trick they were all laughing at— knew the joke that even he was laughing at. They were all doing it to trick him, to get him there, right there at that place in that moment. He had to be there, right at that time and that place. He had to be there. It was very important and they had all tricked him to get him there.

All to get Murphy there to see the man's thumb, the man he knew in the shadows, to see the man's thumb pull the hammer of the long Colt back and his finger go white at the tip as the man squeezed the trigger.

Then slowly, so slowly, Murphy pulled the Smith up but knew, knew that even if he got a round off, it would do no good.

Now the Colt recoiled in the man's hand, up and back to the right, and belched a great cloud of smoke. Murphy saw the hammer drop and the powder ignite. Saw it all. Saw the smoke come out the sides of the cylinder and saw the round nose of death—the round nose of the bullet—leave the barrel of the Colt and cross the room.

Oh, he thought. Oh. It is for *me.* That is for *me.*

Round death. The bullet slid across, shining in the light from the lamps, a yellow-silver shine on its nose. It took him just above the belt buckle, just above the low button on his vest. He looked down to see the tiny puff of dust as it went in and thought—that is my life.

That puff of dust when the bullet hit was my life leaving. He went back and down with the slug, watched his boots come up in front of him, his legs and boots come up and feel the floor. He hit his back and saw the lamp hanging from the ceiling overhead. He knew he was dying. Knew that it was over and done. And knew the man, then. Knew the man with the .45 long Colt.

Murphy woke up in sweat, always, without making the name. Only knowing that he knew the man. Each time Murphy was not sure if this time it was real or still a dream; not sure if the bullet was really in him.

Murphy came to on the bench near the door, his left hand clutching his stomach, his vest and shirt knotted in his fist, his right hand down on his Smith, his revolver half out of the holster.

Pain. Stomach pain.

I'm alive, he thought. I'm still alive. There is no bullet. It was a dream.

He was lying on his side, so he slid over and let his legs lift him up, wiped his mouth with the back of his hand, and pulled out his watch.

Just after five. Only two hours of sleep. The

dream always shook him, but this time it seemed worse—something to do with Sarah. He stood, stretched out some of the kinks from the oak bench, which had been a church pew before a lamp fire claimed the Methodist church, and looked out the window.

First light. Midge would be putting coffee on now, kindling the stove, and starting coffee. But it wouldn't be ready for another hour. Milt must still be on the street. Good.

Murphy walked to the pitcher and basin near the stove. There was enough water to rinse out his mouth and spit out the door. He ran his fingers through his hair, felt knots, said ". . . to hell with it," and put his hat on. He could go to his room later and clean up, but something had come to him just as he dozed off; he wanted to work on it.

He went to his desk and pulled out a pencil and a lined school tablet. The pencil was dull. He sharpened it with his penknife. Then he began to write about Sarah. He started with the time of day he thought the crime had happened—in his mind he thought of it now only as "the crime." Not in detail. He could not think in detail without suffering. It couldn't have happened the night before because she would have been missed. So it probably was early in the morning.

Early in the morning she had gone out to play. Somebody had come by, or called to her, or enticed her to the livery. No. That didn't work. The man wouldn't try to take her to the livery because he would think Old Colonel was there, as he was. Something else took her to the livery.

Maybe she saw a cat or a kitten at the stable. Or it might have been a colt. There was a mare in back with a colt. Something cute brought her from her yard, perhaps. And she went to the stable and he, whoever he was, saw her and followed her.

It's working now, he thought, writing.

The man saw her and followed her into the livery. The opportunity was there, and the son-of-a-bitch went crazy with it . . . no. The man wouldn't do that because Old Colonel was there; the man would figure Old Colonel was there.

But what if the man didn't know Old Colonel was there until the man was done? How would that work? Suppose the man followed her to the livery, thought he was alone with her, dragged her into the manger, and . . .

That worked. And after it was done the man discovered Old Colonel. But could the man have done that without making enough noise to bring Old Colonel down from the hayloft?

Damn. There had to be noise to it. She had to have screamed.

Murphy didn't know enough. Not yet. He wrote it all down but he didn't know enough. He would have to ask Doc about Sarah some more, and about Old Colonel.

Murphy needed to know more.

The door to the office opened. Murphy looked up. Milt said, "Good. You're up. You'd better come out here."

"What's the matter?"

"I don't know. Strangest damn thing I ever saw. Come here and look."

Murphy went out with Milt and looked up the street.

At the other end of town, just at the edge of the last building before the livery, a horse came walking. Or trying to walk. The horse was staggering, with his front legs spread wide and his back legs working almost independently of each other.

"What the hell?"

"I don't know. I was coming over here to make coffee and wake you up, when I looked up and saw him coming. It's taken him all this time to make a hundred yards or so, wobbling and spread that way. He looks hurt, hurt bad."

Murphy started up the street. There was no rider, but the horse was saddled, Murphy could see that. The horse was a big buckskin, close to sixteen hands. Murphy recognized it as one of the livery rentals. Old Colonel had picked the horse up off a busted cowboy six, seven months ago. It was an all right horse but Murphy didn't like buckskins. He thought they drew flies because they were too light; a light horse drew flies. He remembered as he walked toward the animal that the teamster who had seen Wil said Wil had been riding a buckskin.

That meant Wil had rented a horse yesterday morning, then ridden out of town. Which put Wil in the livery yesterday morning, early. Which, Murphy thought, put Wil in a very bad place to be yesterday morning.

The buckskin staggered to the livery door and stopped just as they walked up to him.

"Good Lord!" Milt said. "Look at him!"

Murphy was looking but couldn't believe it either. The horse was laid open from his front shoulder, just in front of the saddle, all the way down his back and across one rump muscle. It was a huge, gaping wound—a massive tear, four feet long, filled with flies and welling blood. In some places Murphy could see through the membrane on the ribs, see the guts inside.

The horse should be dead, Murphy thought. It's impossible that the horse could be alive with that wound. Let alone walking. No, not walking, staggering, falling forward.

"He's in bad shock and awful pain," Milt said. "I think we should put him out of his misery."

Murphy nodded. Milt shot the horse once, in back of the ear.' That ended it. They pulled at the saddle and examined the wound.

"I once saw a horse cut bad by a lion that dropped out of a tree and tore him up some. But it was nothing like this. Nothing this bad. What could have caused this?"

Murphy thought he knew but wasn't sure. He

followed the wound to the edge of the saddle, then turned the saddle over and examined the padding. There was a long groove through the sheepskin, a dented groove. "Bullet."

Milt stared. "Just one?"

"I think so. From a big rifle. It came from the left front, went under the saddle and out through the top of the rump. One long gash."

"It had to cut two feet of meat, or more. That's one hell of a rifle."

"Still. It was a bullet. Somebody was shooting at the rider, maybe, and shot a bit low."

"You know," Milt said, "this is coming up on being a real rough town. I only been here four or five days, and I ain't seen nothing but trouble."

Murphy nodded. "Seems to be piling up." But he had something now. An idea. Say Wil had been in the livery and had come on the girl. Say he had been the one. Then he took a horse out of town, taking it slow, not to arouse suspicion. That was working a bit, but it could have happened—Wil was a cool bastard. It didn't figure he was the one to do that to Sarah. He didn't seem the type. But then, who was? Who was? So he gets out of town and somebody follows him. Somebody knows, and follows him, and shoots at him.

That might work.

It worked a lot better when Murphy remembered that two years ago Charley Penches had gone east on the prairie to hunt hides. "Come on."

"Where we going?"

"To talk to Charley Penches. I just remembered that he hunted buffalo two years ago."

"Oh yeah?"

"Yes. He's got a .50–120 Sharps that'll take the wall off an outhouse. And every reason in the world to use it."

CHAPTER 9

THE SUN CAME up over the eastern edge of town
when they got to the Penches house. It was a small
frame house made of clapboard and strip siding,
put up when there was still the smell of paydirt and
lumber cost more than blood. The house would
have been ugly, Murphy thought, anywhere in the
world except Cincherville. Clariss kept the house
and yard spotless and had put up a picket fence.
Where did she get the whitewash for the stakes?
She also had some flowers planted from seeds from
a catalog. The flowers had, somehow, survived—
tiger lilies and other flowers Murphy couldn't name
—bringing color. The house shone compared to
all the other houses in town, and looked almost
pretty.

Just in that yard, Murphy thought as they walked

through the gate, just in that yard two days ago he had seen Sarah playing with a couple of boards she had made into a doll house, sitting on a rock playing . . . He shook his head, went to the door, and knocked softly. Milt stood in back of him. He turned and signed Milt to move to the side a bit. He didn't want the two of them in line. He wanted them apart. If something happened.

Milt nodded and moved as Murphy knocked again, still soft, but a bit harder. Murphy's helper would learn, but didn't know yet, what he would need to survive.

Murphy heard movement in the house. Somebody coughed. Light cough. That would be Clariss. He eased the Smith in his holster and moved to the side a bit more. He didn't want this to be—didn't want to have to think of this with Charley—but he had to be ready.

Heavy steps. Coming from the back. He wondered where they would have the body. Today would be warm. They would have to bury her. Jesus, he thought, listen to me. This job is ruining me, ruining my head.

The door opened and Charley stood there, red eyed. He looked, Murphy thought, just like he'd spent a week in hell. His eyes weren't just red, they were sunken, dead eyes. His hair was tousled, his shirt half unbuttoned, and he was in bare feet. Usually he was a carefully tidy man, as most powder men were—slow and cautious, easy men—but he had lost it in the night.

"Oh," Charley said. "It's you. What do you want?"

"I just want to have a little talk. I hate to bother you, Charley, but something has come up."

For a moment the face quickened. "Have you caught him? Have you caught the bastard?"

Murphy was taken aback at the look on Charley's face; a feral, no, almost canine look. The look of a wolf smelling blood meat. Smelling the kill. With a hot, intense hatred in it—a look that came from his soul; Charley hated with his soul.

"I don't know what we got, Charley. A few minutes ago Wil's rented buckskin came in all shot to hell. We had to put the horse down."

"Oh! I thought I heard a shot. But we were in the back room with . . . with Sarah. Clariss is still there. What did it mean, the horse coming in that way?"

Murphy shook his head. "I'm not sure. But I think Wil might have been at the livery yesterday morning."

"Was it him?" Charley looked over his shoulder, stepped outside, and closed the door. "Are you telling me it was Wil Jamison?"

Again Murphy shook his head. He felt Milt move to his left rear and held up his hand. Charley was close, too close, but this time it was all right. "I don't know what I'm saying. I just think he was there, was there early in the morning, and might have seen something. His horse came back this morning all blown up—had been shot with some kind of big rifle. So I wanted to ask you, Charley, do you still have that .50–120 Sharps? And where were you yesterday after you came into town?"

Charley stared at him. "What did you think, Murphy? Did you think that I found out he was the one, rode out somewhere, and killed him? Is that what you thought? And would you give a good damn if I did? If he was the one, don't I have the right to kill the bastard any way I want to kill him?"

Yes, Murphy thought, but he shook his head. "I don't know, Charley. I'm just trying to sort all this out."

"You've got a lot of bark on your tree to come at me like this, with my daughter lying in the back room of my house. Some blasted bark." But his voice sounded flat, tired. "I wouldn't have your job, if you have to do this kind of thing."

Murphy said nothing, but at that moment agreed with him. This was crazy, asking him. But the hot worm, the question, was still there. It wouldn't go away just because Murphy felt bad. Murphy said nothing, but he waited. Waited, heard Milt cough, and finally Charley shrugged, shrugged all of his life away somehow, shrugged his hate away.

"I was here with Clariss," Charley said, "after I got back from McCormick's. You think I could leave her? Hell . . . she's all broken inside. Broken into pieces."

Murphy nodded and turned to leave, satisfied

that he had asked, not wanting to push it further. But Charley stopped him.

"I don't have the gun anymore. Six, seven months ago, when I wasn't making work, I sold it for bean money."

Murphy waited, finally asked. "You remember who you sold it to?"

A small movement of Charley's lips—not a smile. He was too far gone to smile. With an acceptance of the irony, the blow of life, Charley said, "I sold it to Wil Jamison. He wanted to hang it in the saloon." Charley closed the door—not a slam—but shut tight against Murphy, maybe forever.

Hell, Murphy thought. This isn't working.

He turned and started for the cafe. Milt followed, hurrying to catch up.

"You know," Milt said, "if I had to do that often, I'm not so sure I could stand this work."

Murphy didn't look at him—kept walking. "You can quit any time you want to."

"Sorry."

"Never mind. I'm tired and this whole mess is starting to get to me. Let's eat and have some coffee. My mouth tastes like I've been chewing on your socks."

"I don't have any socks."

"Exactly."

They went into Midge's. Murphy stopped just inside the door. The smell of fresh coffee and potatoes came from the kitchen and wrapped around him like a warm blanket. He had a mental flash of his childhood—not his mother. Never his mother. She never cooked, that he could remember. But there was a woman down a floor in the tenement in the Tenderloin, a fat woman with huge breasts and a housecoat that never closed. She smiled at the small Irish brat in the hall; she cooked potatoes in a big cast iron pan, sliced them thin and fried them crisp sprinkled with pepper.

She always smiled and never once gave him a taste of the potatoes. But how he loved the smell of them.

Midge's potatoes smelled the same. She sliced them thin and used a lot of mail-order pepper on them, cooked them crisp, and kept them on the hot part of the stove until they were seared through. Then she served them with fresh eggs from hens kept by the Chinese family out by the side of town—full, yellow, yolk-rich eggs; they let the hens range rather than feed them only on grain. She served the potatoes with the eggs; the yolks were soft and ran over the potatoes. . . .

Lord, I'm hungry, Murphy thought. Starved.

Midge came from the kitchen, wiping her hands on her apron, and smiled when she saw the two men standing inside the door. A fly had followed them in and went for the kitchen smells. She reached around the kitchen door for the swatter and cut it down with a tiny flick. Then she rehung the swatter. "You want coffee."

Not a question, a statement. Murphy nodded and Milt headed for the table back in the corner, so they could see the door. He was learning. Murphy held the picture of Midge standing in the kitchen doorway for another second after she was gone, the light around her, her hair back in a tie but hanging down her back in a kind of tail, her shoulders angled and gentle, and her full hips.

Unnnhhh. He thought. It won't be long now.

He sat at the table and she brought them coffee. "Eggs for you both? And fries?"

"I'll just eat the kitchen," Milt smiled. "I thought that stew would take me, but now I'll just eat the whole kitchen."

She laughed, low and soft, but she was looking at Murphy. Then she went back into the kitchen.

"There's a dead horse out there," Murphy said, "if you're really hungry."

Milt grimaced, remembering. "What are we going to do about that?"

"We aren't going to do anything about it. You are going to handle it, right after we eat. You take one of the big bays out of the livery, some harness, and a singletree, and jerk that carcass around to the back of town—before it gets too warm. The coyotes and dogs will clean it up in a day or so."

Milt nodded. "I'll feed the livery stock and water them too. No sense letting them suffer."

Murphy thought a moment. "Come to that, we might as well keep renting them. Just scribble a sign and put a half-gallon bucket for people to drop money in. You don't have to stay there, but anybody who wants to rent a horse can get one that way. They'll cheat, but most of them will throw something in the can. Enough for hay—and maybe to bury Old Colonel and get him a board or stone. When you get that done I want you to do a little investigating."

Milt took a sip of coffee, put a little more sugar in it, and swallowed big. "The rifle, right?"

Murphy raised his eyebrows. "You are quick, aren't you?"

"It had to follow. The horse was hit with something big. If we can find that rifle, it might be the one."

"So you try to find it."

"Right. I'll start at the saloon and see if it's there—ask around town. Somebody might know where it is if it isn't at the saloon."

"You might also clean the office, if you get time."

"If I get time." Milt put his empty cup down. "What are you going to be doing, if it's not rude to ask the boss?"

"Not rude at all. I'm going to saddle that sorrel of mine and go for a ride—too nice a day to spend in town." Murphy turned as Midge came from the kitchen with two plates of potatoes and eggs. "See if I can backtrack that horse—look for Wil Jamison. I don't know how long it will take. Oh, one more thing."

"What's that?"

Murphy waited until Midge was back in the

kitchen, then leaned over and spoke softly. "There's two or three families, I guess, four, with kids. I want you to go around to their houses, polite and all, and tell them to keep their kids to home and watch them close for a while, until we get this sorted out. Not that they'd need telling after yesterday."

Milt nodded, took a mouthful of eggs and potatoes, and then frowned. "You don't think they'll mind, not knowing who I am and all?"

Murphy smiled. "Hell, this is a small town. Everybody knew who you were ten minutes after I put you on."

CHAPTER 10

THEY WALKED TOGETHER to the livery, and Murphy helped Milt get one of the bays into a harness. They got two wrong size collars before they found the right size hanging on pegs in the tack room. Then they had to let a harness out to fit the bay. Murphy thought for a moment about taking a buggy—Old Colonel had one at the side of the livery barn. If Murphy did find something, which he doubted, he could carry it back that way. But he decided against it. "Never follow a horse with a buggy," he often said. All the tracks had to do was turn into the breaks or the foothills, and he would have to turn the buggy back. Worse, he might throw a spoke or bust a rim on a rock, then he would have to ride the harness horse home bareback.

Murphy took his sorrel and threw a couple of

pounds of oats in a feed sack. On second thought
he went back to the cafe while Milt was snatching
the carcass out of town and had Midge make him
up a couple of sandwiches for his saddlebags. She
wrapped them in wax paper and put them in a flour
sack—two roast beef sandwiches from a cold roast
in the cream cooler on the back porch—and he
thanked her.

The sorrel was a little froggy, and he jumped two
or three times. But Murphy was heavy on him, and
he settled fast. Murphy ran for a mile, maybe a bit
more, to loosen his crotch and get out of town
before somebody saw him and started asking questions. It was still early, but the town was starting to
come around. There were people moving; Milt
could handle them.

It struck Murphy then that he had only put Milt
on the day before and was already depending on
him. Milt was a fast learner and would make a good
man. To be a sheriff . . .

To be a sheriff.

What was that to be? Murphy's gold—to be a
sheriff. He ought to fire Milt and save him grief.
Murphy pulled the sorrel in, into a trot and down
to a fast walk. He had no idea how far he would
have to go, but he didn't want to blow the horse
early.

There was a trail to follow. He started out on the
road to McCormick's, and soon he began to see
flecks of blood left by the buckskin as it had
staggered down the road. His sorrel, smelling the

blood as well, kept his head skittish, ears flapping like a windmill and eyes rolling.

"Come on, dummy," Murphy swore, but with some affection. He was beginning to like the sorrel, for all his bad trotting. Murphy wasn't sure if he liked the horse because he was a decent horse or because Murphy had been stupid enough to spend two hundred dollars on him and was trying to justify the deal. "Settle in, settle in."

The blood was sporadic, as if the wound on the buckskin had opened and closed, and Murphy had to watch close for the drops in the dust. It was impossible to follow just tracks. There were too many of them in the ruts from freight wagons going back and forth from McCormick's. But he kept seeing the tiny flecks of blood, and it kept him going.

Six miles out of town, on a bit more, still almost three miles from the McCormick hole, he realized that he had gone for a time without seeing blood. He halted the sorrel, got off, and walked ahead leading the horse, looking more closely.

Nothing.

He stopped and stood, looking around, although he didn't know for sure what he expected to see. The blood had either diminished or the horse had gone for a time without bleeding. Hard to believe either—that it had gone without bleeding, or that the bleeding had stopped altogether.

He took his hat off. Midmorning now. He'd been moving slowly, following the track. It had taken him the morning to go six miles. The sun was high enough to be hot. His forehead was sweaty and he could smell himself. He needed a bath at Harry's hotel and a change of clothes. He needed to be able to figure this out. He needed lots of things. He needed some time sitting alone on a porch swing with a cold beer and Midge next to him.

"Hell," he snorted. When had he ever sat on a porch swing with a girl? Cribs in cowtowns, fast sweat, stink—never a porch swing.

He looked up the road, felt the sorrel move impatiently, and smiled at him. A good horse wanted to move. Somebody had said that to him once—who was that? Oh, yeah. Old Colonel had said it, "a good horse wants to move." The sorrel rubbed a fly off his shoulder, and Murphy turned and scratched the horse between the ears. Might be an all-right horse.

Murphy climbed back up and settled into the saddle, then kneed the sorrel up the road for another half a mile, looking for blood. Nothing. Still nothing.

He turned and headed back the way he had come. The sorrel thought they were going home and started to run, but Murphy fought him down. The horse kept jumping ahead and finally Murphy had to get off and walk, leading him. Perhaps that buckskin had come onto the road from the side, and Murphy had missed the turning place.

And he almost missed it again.

He walked nearly a mile, sick of walking, but

afraid that if he rode again he would miss something. Just as he was passing a small wash, dried and dead for years, he saw a scuff to the side, well off the road.

He mounted and turned up the wash. The sorrel, mad because he wasn't going home, frogged sideways for a hundred feet. Murphy pulled in tight. Fifty or sixty yards up the wash he saw a spot of blood and knew he was on the track again.

The tracks headed straight up the wash, west, toward the mountains in the distance. The wash quickly leveled, and Murphy found himself riding across rolling foothills, following the blood, which was a steady line now, a steady brown line where the blood had dried.

It was amazing how far the horse had come, amazing how much blood there was in a horse. In two miles, almost two and a half, the trail turned again and went off to the north for half a mile, then headed west again. Murphy began to think he had misread it or had it wrong, that the horse couldn't have come this far, even down the mountain, not with that wound.

Then ahead a half a mile on a bald hill, he saw the remains of a cabin, an old prospector's shack. Overhead two buzzards circling, getting lower; he knew he was still right.

He rode another quarter mile, then stopped and got off. He didn't know what to expect, but he wasn't going to ride in sitting up straight and pretty for anybody to sight on, either.

He pulled his Smith, held it at his side, and led the sorrel as he walked to the cabin, his thumb on the hammer. The buzzards circled higher and moved away. When he was a hundred yards from the shack a coyote ran off to the side.

Fifty yards from the shack he stopped and looked at the ground. He was standing in the middle of an immense smear of blood, two or three feet wide and five feet long. This must be where the horse was shot. The bullet would have carried blood and horseflesh out from the strike. He looked at the angle and realized that the bullet had come from the direction of the shack. Somebody sitting in the shack had waited until the horse was fifty yards away, then blew half its back open trying to shoot Wil Jamison.

With his own rifle?

Well, hell. There was more than one big gun in the world, wasn't there?

He continued to the shack, half expecting to find a body, but there wasn't one. Not even any blood. The old shack was barren and empty, half the roof gone, with part of a table in one corner. Nothing else. He was turning to go back outside when a glint of metal caught his eye, and he leaned back in, under the table, and saw two cartridge cases.

He snaked them out with his arm and knew them immediately, without having to study their backs. They were long, half-inch brass tubes—both of them for a .50–120 Sharps.

Well, he thought. Well. That narrowed it down a

bit. There couldn't be that many in all of Colorado, let alone Cincherville. It had to be the one Charley owned. Had to be.

But two of them? Two shots?

Of course, he thought. Of course. The first one missed, went between Jamison's legs, whistled his nuts, and set the horse back and down. Jamison probably got off, took to running, and was shot again. Two shots.

But where was Jamison?

Murphy went back out into the sun, untied the sorrel from the wall boards of the shack, and mounted. Just do a circle. About fifty yards out in the rocks and grass start doing a circle.

As it worked out he didn't have to finish the first loop. In some rocks a hundred yards to the rear of the shack he saw a coyote go running. He dismounted again, approached cautiously, and found him, found Wil Jamison.

He was sitting with his back to a rock, his head slumped forward on his chest, and his hat at his side in the dirt. A black hat with a silver hat band that looked like a solid silver belt. Always was a flashy bastard, Murphy thought.

In Jamison's right hand was a Colt, draped across his leg. For a heartbeat Murphy thought of his dream, saw the Colt come up, and at him, but it didn't move, just hung there between Jamison's legs.

From the waist down Jamison was a mass of

blood. It was hard to tell because of the mess, but it looked like he'd been hit through the hips, sideways. "Hell of a wound," Murphy mumbled aloud, grimacing at the pain it must have caused. He looked back to reconstruct the events and found a blood spot twenty feet away, not as big as a horse but large, perhaps one foot by three feet. Then he saw a smear where the bullet had taken Jamison down, then a sliding scrabble-trail where Jamison had dragged himself to the rocks for cover.

Like an animal.

Murphy looked back at the cabin and saw, from the angle of the initial impact smear, that whoever did the shooting was probably still in the shack. Cool bastard, reloaded and caught Jamison just as he got to the rocks. One shot.

And then didn't come to finish him. Why?

Murphy turned back to Jamison, reached down, pulled the Colt loose—Jamison's fingers weren't in rigor, which Murphy thought was strange—opened the loading gate, eared it to half cock, and spun the cylinder. Every round was fired.

Jamison had gotten to the rocks, got his gun out, and fired back over the top of the rocks. Probably hadn't hit anything, probably couldn't hit anything, but the firing would have scared the other one off, kept him from coming to finish the job with Jamison's own rifle.

With Jamison's own rifle.

"Nnnnnnnnggggghhh . . ."

The sound cut the still noon air like a wet knife and scared the breath out of Murphy. For a second he couldn't place it, only knew that it went inside him.

Then he realized it was from Jamison.

Somehow, some incredible way, Jamison was still alive.

CHAPTER 11

MURPHY WENT TO Jamison's side and knelt next to him. There was no movement. At first Murphy couldn't even see breathing, but when he felt the inside of Jamison's neck there was a faint pulse. There was life, some life inside the bleeding hulk. Murphy whispered in his ear, not knowing why he whispered.

"Do you know who did this to you? Who did this, Jamison?"

No sound now. Jamison could not live much longer, and he could not be moved. The pain of being moved would finish him. Murphy also knew he could not give Jamison water; he could see guts in the wound. In the army they said never give food or water to somebody hit in the stomach.

So there was only one way for this to go. Jamison

could stay here and Murphy could go for Doc Hensley, in which event Jamison would be dead before Murphy got back. Or Murphy could stay, make it as comfortable for Jamison as possible, and hope that he said something before he died.

Murphy chose the latter and went to his horse for his poncho. He weighted the edge of it with rocks, propped it over Jamison with two sticks to provide shade—the sun was cooking down on him—then used the tail of his shirt to moisten Jamison's lips with water. That brought the first hint of movement, the only hint Murphy was to see. The tip of Jamison's tongue crept out of the corner of his mouth and found the moisture, like a snake, then went back in. Murphy put more water there but the tongue didn't come out again, and Jamison fell silent.

By looking closely Murphy could see Jamison's chest rising and falling, but the breathing was very shallow and quick. Murphy knew that the shock would only deepen and deepen until Jamison was dead.

Still he waited. Murphy sat next to the dying man for all of the afternoon, asking periodically if he could identify who had shot him, but Jamison only made one more sound. Not in answer to a specific question, but out of nowhere, he said something that sounded like he was trying to make a word.

"Haaarrrnnnn."

And that was it. If it was part of a name or identity, it made no sense to Murphy. And there wasn't anything else. Murphy checked his watch at four o'clock. About ten minutes after that Jamison died without moving or making any other sounds. The shallow breathing simply stopped. Murphy felt for a pulse in the neck, found none, and stood.

"You were tougher than I thought you could be," he said, by way of a compliment. He could have said death words or burying words over Jamison, but he didn't know them or believe in them. Instead, he stretched the body on the ground, rolled it in the poncho, and draped it over the sorrel in back of the cantle.

The horse went half-hermantile on him, threw Jamison's body off twice, but Murphy swore, popped the horse and finally he stopped jumping around. Then Murphy got on him and started home, taking it slow and easy because of the heavy load.

It was a long ride home; Murphy had a lot to chew on.

Milt was at the office when Murphy rode in just at dark.

"Jamison?" Milt pointed at the body in the tarp.

Murphy nodded. "We'll take him up to Doc's and get him ready for burying. He's blown up pretty bad. Somebody shot him with the same gun as they used on that damn horse, a .50–120. I found two cartridge cases. Did you learn anything about the rifle?"

Milt shook his head. "Not yet. And I think I've asked everybody. But the rifle is gone—it's not in the saloon. Although Skeeter did say that Jamison had bought it from Charley, so that checks out."

"I figured it would."

"Yeah. But I'm glad. I wasn't looking forward to helping you on Charley Penches."

"Take the body to Doc's, will you? Then take the sorrel over to the livery for some oats. I grained him a bit today while I was waiting for . . . while I was waiting. But he could use half a pound or so. I'm going to get a bath and change some clothes. Then eat. Oh, if you want some sandwiches there are two that I didn't eat in the bags Midge made for me. Grab yourself a bite and a nap, and I'll watch things for a while."

"Couple of things to tell you first."

"What?"

Milt had the reins to the sorrel and rubbed the horse's neck. "The Merchant's Association is having a meeting at eight o'clock tomorrow night over to the drygoods store. They requested your presence."

"I'll bet."

"Well, pretty much ordered it, I guess."

"Right," Murphy sighed. His crotch hurt from riding forward, away from the body, all the way to town. The stink of Jamison's blood had mixed with

Murphy's sweat-stink. He was getting sick of stinking. "What else?"

"There's a couple of riders came in today and have been drinking and making dirt talk at the saloon. I'm not sure what they are, but they ain't cowboys, and they ain't miners. They're both carrying sideguns, and one of them has a Winchester in his saddle boot."

"What do you mean, 'dirt talk'?"

Milt shrugged. "Just that. Talking dirty about women, what they've done with saloon women, that kind of thing. They're both bragging about how Fat Marge couldn't handle them, how it took a whole house full in Abilene—crap like that. I figured it wouldn't mean much, except for what's happened here, and that they aren't just riders and have guns, and the guns are oiled, and so are their holsters—you know what I mean. Like somewhere there might be paper on them. I've been watching them all afternoon, going in now and then, but they haven't done anything except swear and spit and scare people, so I left them alone."

"There are some posters in the office . . ."

"I know. I checked them. But hell, those drawings are pretty much useless, and names change like horses. I didn't recognize them. They told Skeeter they were heading up north to work for some cattleman in Wyoming who was having trouble with squatters, but that don't mean much. Every dumb kid with a gun is going up there to shoot farmers. These look meaner than that, just on the wrong side ... I don't know ... just mean."

"They got names?"

Milt shook his head. "I heard one call the other Jake, but that's all."

I need this, thought Murphy. Couple of hard cases coming into town right about now—I really need this. "Well. It still holds. Get some sleep and I'll watch things for a while."

He watched Milt lead the sorrel up the street to Doc's, the body draped across it bouncing. Something was nagging at Murphy, something that wouldn't go away.

Damn. The body, of course. He never did go through Jamison's pockets. There might be something in there. "Wait. Hold it up."

He walked to the sorrel and threw back the tarp. The shirt pockets had nothing, and he dug gingerly in the pants pockets—the slug had gone through just below the pocket line—to also find nothing. Some change and a pocketknife. But the saloon owner had worn a frock coat as well, and in the inside pocket of the frock coat Murphy found a derringer—a brute of a little gun that took a short .44 cartridge and had two barrels—which Murphy dropped in his pocket. And a piece of paper. It was folded and a bit bloodstained, but Murphy opened it to find a printed deed form, one of the blank deed forms they used to assign property. All the whereases and whereats were printed in so clerks wouldn't have to print them by hand, but the actual land descriptions and names of owners were left blank for the purchasers to fill in. Except that in this case only a land description was written. It was in plain English: ". . . my lands west of the McCormick road between Cincherville and the McCormick mines." In the blank for the name of the buyer was scribbled "Wilton Jamison, Esq." The name of the seller was blank.

Esquire, Murphy thought. That was the day. He waved Milt on and went back into the office, put the deed paper in the drawer of his desk, and let it slip from his mind. Something to check on later. Probably not something to do with this mess, at any rate.

At the hotel he stopped in the lobby. Harry was at the desk and looked up when he came in. "Evening."

Murphy nodded. "Need a hot bath. You got any water fired up?" Harry had a bath house on the back of the hotel, a clapboard room with a stock tank for a tub and a wood-fired water heater outside, hooked to a pump. Baths were a quarter but worth it, Murphy thought, when you stink like me.

"The heater still has coals, so it won't take much. Maybe twenty minutes." Harry stood up from his stool in back of the desk. "Is that all right?" He wanted to ask more. Murphy could see it in his eyes. Harry wanted to ask questions about all the things that had been going on because Harry liked to talk, and he wanted Murphy to give him something to talk about. But he saw how tired the sheriff was, saw the edge in his eyes, and didn't ask anything more.

Murphy nodded and went to the stairs leading up to his room. His home. He stopped with his boot on the first step and turned to Harry. "There are a couple of new riders just come into town. Have they registered here?"

Harry shook his head. Short, bald, and round, he looked always on the edge of turning into an elf. "I heard they were over at the saloon drinking hammers, but that's all. They aren't signed up here."

As if there was another hotel in town, Murphy thought. If they were drinking hammers—straight double whiskeys with a beer chaser—they would be drunk soon. Either mean drunk or passed-out drunk, although they sounded from Milt like they would be mean drunks. "Twenty minutes is fine."

Murphy went upstairs and into his room. The bed was made. Harry paid Won-Cho to come in every morning and straighten up the rooms. So the bed was made and it looked awfully good. Murphy thought about saying to hell with the bath and catching a couple of hours of lay-down sleep but knew if his head hit the pillow, he would be out for the night.

He stripped off his shirt and threw it in the corner basket for Won-Cho. She also did laundry, owned a mine out of town, and in general supported her husband, who liked to farm and raise chickens and vegetables. Or they supported each other, Murphy thought. They lived and worked with each other. Not just together, but fit to each other, like a good team fit each other. Like he thought it might be with Midge . . .

Murphy found the pint of whiskey in the stand under the pitcher and bowl, took a mouthful straight from the bottle, sloshed it around to cut the dust out of his mouth, and spit out the back window without swallowing. It was cheap, barrel whiskey, but it took the stink of Jamison's blood out of Murphy's nose and mouth, and that was something. He didn't swallow because that might make him dull off a bit. He didn't want to be dull right now. Maybe not ever, but, for sure, not right now.

Harry called up that the water was hot. Murphy carried fresh clothes, his razor, strop, and gunbelt down the back stairs to the bath-house. Inside, he shaved, only cutting himself three times—there was too much face. When it slid straight in one place it always seemed to pull sideways in another, and he'd cut himself. After shaving, he sat into the tub, his gun close, hanging on the back of a chair.

I'm turning into an old woman, he thought, looking at the gun. Getting too safe.

But he kept thinking of the way the bullet had gone across the hips on Jamison, like some kind of giant sledge had hit him sideways. And the bullet that laid the horse open. He thought maybe he didn't have enough gun. There was a Greener in the office, an old double-twelve with curled hammers, that fired black powder loads through a twist barrel. He had cut it off to sixteen inches and shot double-ought buck in it, nine balls to a shell. After forty yards it spread so bad you could drive a team through it, but in close it packed a hell of a wallop.

Maybe he'd start carrying the Greener around at night. Or have Milt do it.

That ought to set the good citizens of Cincherville on their ear. Find their old-woman sheriff running around with a Greener, afraid of the dark.

And that is just the problem, he thought, sitting in the tub with steam coming up.

I am afraid of the dark.

CHAPTER 12

When his bath was done Murphy dressed all in fresh clothes, down to his skin, and went to Midge's. As soon as he was in the door, he wished he hadn't come. Sitting at the back were the four leading merchants, or businessmen, in town.

Like a pack of dogs chewing at a bone, Murphy thought, as he walked in and stood to the side of the door. He almost turned and went out, but it was a very small town. He'd have to face them at the meeting later, anyway.

The point is, he thought, that I don't respect them or like them. They got no sand. Nothing in their sack.

"Gentlemen." Murphy said it straight, even. "Come out for supper?" Usually they ate at home with their families.

107

Hardesty, the banker, with a sheen of sweat on his face; Grimm, from the hardware and harness store; Erickson, who owned the freight office; and Shannon, who ran the general mining supply warehouse—all the money in town.

All the money in town.

Hardesty was the only one who really looked the part, though. He had a gut but covered it with a plain brown vest, with a small gold chain across for his watch. He had a little bit of flesh to his cheeks but not too much, sideburns, and a trimmed mustache and hair. He looked like what Murphy thought a banker should look like. Nicest house in town, with real lap siding, painted with real white paint. And the bank, Cincherville National, was made of real bricks and had a real concrete-mount safe. Son-of-a-bitch wore a Stetson, Murphy thought, that cost more than I make in a month.

Hardesty beckoned to him and Murphy leaned over the table. There was nobody else in the cafe except the other three. Midge was back in the kitchen. But Hardesty whispered anyway.

"We were just discussing this . . . unfortunate affair."

Murphy studied him. "You mean the rape and murder of a small girl, the murder of the livery man, and the murder of the saloon owner?" Murphy did it on purpose and saw shots when Hardesty winced.

"Yes. Well. We are getting a little concerned."

"I suppose you are. Couple more days there

won't be anybody left in town, the rate they're getting killed." Murphy looked around the room, back to the table. "Where's Jensen? Shouldn't he be here with you?"

"Randy had books to do, but he'll be there tomorrow night at the meeting. You're coming, aren't you?"

It's not as if I had a choice, is it, Murphy thought. But he nodded. "I'll be there."

"We would like a progress report then."

"You would." Not a question, a statement.

"Unless you could tell us now. You know, if you're making any progress on this thing?"

Murphy stood erect and eased his belt, watching their eyes—all of them—follow his hands down to his gun. There was concern, he knew, but there was something else in the room. They had been talking something else when he came in. They wanted to know more. They were more than worried. They were afraid. But more, still more, they were curious.

They had a greasy curiosity, Murphy thought. "I don't have anything I want to talk about in a public cafe."

"But there is some progress?" Hardesty pushed. Something's there, Murphy thought, something in the corners of his brown eyes making him push.

Murphy nodded. "There are pieces. They are falling in together. You could say that."

Hardesty nodded, his mouth slightly open and damp at the corner, breathing through his nose, waiting, waiting. His eyes were speculative, rigid in the corners. "I think you're playing with us. I don't think you have anything."

Careful, Hardesty, Murphy thought. Be very careful now. It is too soon since Sarah. "Believe what you like."

"I believe if you had anything, you'd tell us."

"Believe what you want," Murphy repeated.

Midge came from the kitchen with a tray full of coffee for the table. Murphy used it as a way to break away. He went to the other side of the room, the farthest table he could get, sat, and waited.

Midge came to the table. "Are you eating?"

"You have flour on your cheek."

"Are you sure it isn't face powder set there on purpose?"

He shook his head. "You don't wear powder and there's close to a pound of it."

Across the room the four men were talking, huddled forward. Murphy ignored them. "I'll have the special."

"I've got some second day stew, always better than first. Your deputy liked it."

"He was in, was he?"

She nodded. "Hour ago. Said he liked those beef sandwiches I made for you and then ate a full meal. He must be hollow."

Murphy felt bad about the sandwiches. But with Jamison that way he didn't feel much like eating. Too many smells. "I'm sorry but it wasn't a day for eating."

"I heard. Too bad about Jamison. I mean he wasn't much, but you don't wish that on anybody. Was . . . was he the one?"

Murphy rubbed his face. The whole day was coming on him. He shook his head. "I don't think so."

Midge sighed and wiped her hands on her apron. "We went two, three years without a death like this—not even drunks at the saloon. And now, in five or six days. What's the matter with this place?"

"Maybe it's time to move on."

She shrugged. "But where do you go? Where do you go in this country?"

"Charley Penches was after going back East and getting a farm—before this happened. A farm with green grass to it. Maybe that doesn't sound so bad."

"Is that what you want—to be a farmer?"

There it was—the open question. What did he want to do? Her eyes were frank, clear, waiting. "I don't know," he said, and he meant it.

She turned and in a few minutes brought back a plate of stew with potatoes and carrots cooked down to soft. He agreed, second day stew was better than first. When he was half done eating the four men got up and left, and he was alone with her. She came back out of the kitchen with two cups of coffee and sat at the table.

Two or three times a week they sat alone and talked, but in the past four days there had not been time. They didn't talk about anything important, usually, but Murphy had come to look forward to their sits. The cafe was quiet, with the soft light from the oil lamps on the walls—it was peace for Murphy. Some of the only peace he got. It somehow gave him room.

"Do you want to talk?" she asked.

He shook his head. "I'll listen."

"Well, let's see what to tell you. I'm making a new dress. I got some pretty, print material with flowers on it, tight little flowers, from mail order . . . you don't want to hear this, do you?"

But he nodded. "Yes. Very much."

So she talked of her life. He listened, didn't ignore it, but listened and marvelled at the life she had made in this town, at the beauty and settled nature she had carved out of the middle of a stinking, dead, boom town; marvelled at how she spread that beauty, shared it, and could not believe in the ugly things.

It lifted him out of himself, and when he left, half an hour later, a part in the center of him had decided that he had to talk to Midge about the crime. About later. About what there would be after he had settled all this—about there being two people and not just one. He had decided that they could live together, that it would work, and that he could quit sheriffing and go to something else. What? Farming, maybe. Maybe that wasn't too bad. Just living. Live like Won-Cho and her husband. Live and smile at the days that he had. Just live. He thought all of that while she was speaking of her life. He was thinking of it when he left the cafe and thinking of her later, as he walked his rounds, thinking all the soft things there would be between them.

And the thinking damn near killed him.

He walked by the office again before doing the rounds and saw Milt sleeping on the bench with a cell blanket over him, left him there quietly, and checked the town, fronts and backs. It was about ten o'clock on the first round. Jensen was just blowing out his lamps and closing. He locked the door as Murphy came by.

"Evening." Murphy slowed, didn't stop.

"You coming tomorrow night?" Jensen asked, standing in the near dark. There was still some glow light from Midge's—and down the street a bit the front windows of the saloon. Noise came from the saloon. Coarse noise.

"I'll be there." Murphy remembered that Jensen had been speaking in Midge's about Sarah. When was that? Two, three days ago. Ten years ago?

"Been here all day?"

"Where else?"

Murphy tried to see Jensen's boots, looking for a cut in the toe, but it was too dark. Besides, talk didn't mean he was the one. Hell, Murphy thought, nothing meant anything anymore with something like that. Jensen said good night and left, and Murphy finished his rounds.

Up in House Street, Murphy could see lights. Hardesty walked by a window in his home, his bulk cutting the light. Then his lights went out. Down the road the others blew out their lamps while Murphy watched. Except for Midge's and the saloon, the town was dark.

I could be doing that, he thought. I could turn in this damned badge, blow Midge's lamp out, and go to bed.

But not yet. He couldn't quit yet. Just one more thing to do. Had to find the son-of-a-bitch who did Sarah. Then he would, he'd turn it over.

The noise from the saloon grew louder, some swearing, and then the unmistakable scream of somebody in pain and the crashing of a fight.

He ran across the street, pulling the Smith as he ran, stopped at the side of the door, and looked around the corner, taking the room into his eyes and holding it, then ducking back.

There was a fight back at the card table, three men hitting each other. One man, one of the regular card players, was back against the wall holding his hand. Blood was dripping down from his wound. Murphy couldn't tell what kind of wound. Maybe knife. One of the strangers was in the fight by the card table. Skeeter was standing behind the bar. Two other men were against the left wall. Clyde was standing with a beer in his hand. Murphy didn't see the other stranger.

Didn't see him.

He said to hell with it and rolled into the room. "That's it! Cool it down, cool it down."

Which of course did nothing, and would not

have mattered, except that it stopped one of the card players in midswing. He took a blow from a billiard cue that caved in half his head. Murphy checked his rear and still couldn't find the other stranger. But you went with what you had. He took four quick strides down the bar and started jerking collars and bashing heads.

Once somebody had given him a dime novel about Jesse James. It was full of the most ridiculous hogwash Murphy ever read. About how Jesse let lawmen draw first and shoot first, about him giving money to the poor. God, it went on and on. But it was worst when the writer—was it Ned something? —had written about a so-called gun battle between Jesse and Frank and a posse that caught them in a saloon. The writer had them coolly taking aim, pacing their shots, and squeezing the rounds off.

It never happened that way. When it came it was fast and tight and dirty, with smoke and noise and the flat metallic taste-smell of fear and death in your mouth, quick breathing, and trying to get as many bullets as possible in the air at once—that's what Murphy thought of fighting with guns.

And when it came this time it was no exception. The stranger in the fight at the card table, a bearded man with a ring on his forehead where his hat-band cut in, heard Murphy yell and turned, drew his pistol, and fired. He had a knife in his left hand, which he had jammed through the hand of the bleeding card player against the wall. With his right hand he drew, reared back, and fired.

Murphy had his gun out, had been using it as a club, and was still completely surprised. No talk, no warning, no indication that it was coming at all. It wasn't the dream. Nobody was laughing. Murphy saw the smoke only after the bullet was already gone, tugging at his head when it passed through his hat brim. Because he was soft, still thinking of quitting, Murphy didn't react until the man had shot twice more.

Twice more the man fired, twice the bullets passed Murphy, the last one actually rubbing his belt as the stranger tried to hit him.

Tried to kill him.

He's trying to kill me.

All fast then. Murphy fell to the right, away from the direction in which the recoil would pull the man's gun, and brought his own gun into line. It was a double action. He fired it as fast as he could, three times, but the first round did it. The bullet took the man almost exactly in the center of the sternum, and he went back and down, dying. Murphy began to straighten but no, not yet, he thought.

Not yet.

And as he thought it, the door to the crib room overhead opened, and the second man came out naked with a gun in his hand, aiming down, jerking off a round while he was still moving. That was the only thing that saved Murphy. The bullet cut across Murphy's left shoulder, deep enough to draw blood. Murphy dropped to one knee to make a smaller target and fired the rest of his cylinder, three more shots, double action, at the man on the top of the steps.

The first two missed. Murphy saw the slugs hit the hand rail and chip the wood. The third round took the man in the middle of his forehead, pushing him back into the room on top of the already screaming Marge. And it was done.

It was done.

The room was full of smoke, swearing, Marge screaming upstairs in German—Murphy had not known she was German—the sulphur stink of powder, and sudden silence.

The man on the floor moved slightly but he was clearly dying. He didn't speak but emitted a low, quiet, almost courteous moaning, which reminded Murphy of the sound Jamison had made. Up on the landing all that showed of the other stranger were the bottoms of his bare feet, both black with dirt.

"Damn." Skeeter had been standing all this time—actually only seconds—with a rag in his claw. He automatically wiped the bar as he swore.

Murphy opened the top of the Smith, cleared the empty cartridges, and put in new ones from his belt. His fingers were shaking, and he fought to bring them under control. The sides of his tongue tasted like old pipe stems.

He stepped forward and kicked the gun away from the hand of the man on the floor, his mind working again. Then he went upstairs and made sure the other one was dead. "Anybody know who they were?" Murphy broke the silence.

Skeeter shook his head. "One was Jake—that's all we knew. They've been drinking mean all day. When you brought Wil in we wanted to close the place down, you know, for him. But they wouldn't let us. So we stayed open and they got to playing cards, bad and dumb, getting drunker all the time. Then one of them stuck his knife through Todd's hand after his cards went sour, and you know the rest." Skeeter looked down to where he was still wiping the bar and threw the rag in the corner disgustedly. Then he looked at Murphy. "You're hit."

Murphy looked at his shoulder, surprised at the blood seeping into his shirt. "I felt it tug, but I didn't know it actually cut in. Damn, I hate this."

Milt came running through the doorway at that moment, with his gun in his hand. "What the hell?" He looked at the carnage, at Murphy. "You're hit."

Murphy nodded. "I know. It's a shallow cut."

"Better get over to Doc's. You might get blood poison, the way the shirt goes into it."

Another nod. "You clean up here and find out what you can. I'll be over at Doc's." Murphy turned and went out into the night before they could see him shake. When he had looked down at his shoulder he had seen the dream, had seen where the bullet had plowed across, and he could only think that if it had been a few inches to the right and lower, he would be gone.

Gone.

For nothing but a couple of saddle bums with two much cheap whiskey in them.

Dead and gone.

He was still shaking when he got to Doc's.

CHAPTER 13

"DAMMIT, DOC, WHAT the hell you pouring in there? That hurts."

"You've been shot. You think it would feel good?"

Murphy sat in a chair at the examining table, with his shirt off and his left arm up on the table. The bullet had plowed in, breaking the skin more through compression than actually cutting. It left a gouge a quarter-inch deep and equally wide across the top of his left shoulder. It was a minor wound, if any wound could be considered minor. Infection was a killer—even the smallest infection could rapidly lead to blood poisoning and death. There was no way to stop it if it started, short of amputation. But when the source of the infection was in the trunk of the body, amputation was not a consideration.

An insect bite could kill you. On his way West, when he was a kid, Murphy had ridden on the train. It stopped to change engines in Omaha. During the delay he had taken a short walk and happened to come on a graveyard. One whole section was devoted to children, small stones for small graves. He'd asked Hensley about it once. "Why so many children?" Hensley had said that they were killed by minor infections that went to their brain and destroyed them—dirt in cuts. Small stuff and it killed them.

"I'm just pouring disinfectant in it." The cold liquid dripped down from the wound, made a streak across his chest, and tightened his stomach muscles. Murphy was just going to ask for a towel when the door burst open and Midge flew in.

"I heard you were hit and I . . ." She stopped, staring at the wound. "Is it bad?"

Murphy shook his head. "A scratch. Nothing more." God, he thought—listen to me lie. Nothing more than a scratch. Just to the right and it would have been the end of me. I was so scared I was shaking too much to reload my gun. I want to scream to Midge how frightened I was, how the terror ripped at me. "I'm fine." But I'm not, I'm torn inside by this, by all of it. I just can't say it.

She reached, with a hand still trembling, and touched his cheek. "I wouldn't be real happy if you died, Murphy."

He shook his head. "I wouldn't like it much, either. But don't worry. I'm all right. You go home and I'll be over to talk when I get this wrapped."

She wouldn't go until he promised her, and Doc told her not to worry, as well. Then she went slowly.

"You'd best do something about that," Doc said, when she'd gone.

"You mean the wound?"

"Don't come on dumb with me. I mean Midge. It's time for you to quit this garbage and settle into something good. Like Midge."

"I've been thinking just that, Doc. Just that." He flexed his arm when Hensley finished taping it. "But I want to clear this up first, this whole mess. If I can." The wound was beginning to stiffen and he winced when he put his shirt back on. "Is there anything you can tell me that might help?"

Doc brought out a bottle of whiskey, sipping whiskey, and poured two glasses half-full. "Not too much. I learned nothing more from Sarah's body because they took her. The funeral is tomorrow, by the way. And there wasn't anything to learn from that pile of meat you brought in today. God, what a wound. It reminded me of the Civil War. We used to see men hit two and three times like that, with those big musket balls—fifty, sixty caliber. They'd be all torn to hell and still alive."

Murphy nodded. Then he told Doc all of it. How Jamison had still been alive. The sounds he made.

"Of course it could mean something," Doc said,

when he'd finished. "But the truth is he was probably so far gone into shock that he didn't even know you were there. The pain would have driven everything else out of him."

"It's just grabbing at nothing. I've got nothing. Three dead people, no, five dead people now, and nothing." Murphy frowned. "It's right there. Something is right there and I can feel it, but I can't get a hold on it. It's like trying to grab smoke. This whole thing. Just smoke."

"Well, there isn't much I can do to help you, I'm afraid."

"How about Old Colonel? He was there. He must have seen something, heard something. How could whoever did it get up in the loft with Old Colonel up there holding a fork? Then get the fork away from him, kill him, and still get away without making a hell of a ruckus?"

"There wasn't much about him, either. Except I'm fairly sure he was drunk."

Murphy thought about it. "How drunk?"

"Most of a pint. There was some of it still in his stomach. It looked like he hadn't had time to clear his throat before it was cut."

"Meaning what?"

"Just that. He was drunk. At his age and with his lowered tolerance, a pint would be a full load."

"Was he out?"

"Probably."

"Completely passed out?"

Doc nodded. "He might have been."

Murphy put his vest on, straightened his gun, and got his hat. "So try this for thinking. He was drunk and passed out in the hayloft. Maybe he went up to get hay, sat down for a drink, and passed out. Or maybe he just crawled up there to sleep it off. That doesn't matter. Down below the man did Sarah, then heard something in the loft, or thought he ought to check it out. He climbed up and saw Old Colonel passed out in the hay. The fork was handy, probably sticking up right there, and he took it and stuck Old Colonel. Then, maybe not sure he was dead, he cut Old Colonel's throat to make sure."

"From the front," Doc said. "That means the killer probably wasn't left-handed."

"That's good." Murphy frowned. "I haven't been able to think of anybody in town who is left-handed. And I haven't found a notched boot, either."

"What's a notched boot have to do with it?"

Murphy quickly told him about the line in the dirt. "I guess I'm not much good at solving mysteries. All my evidence hasn't given me anything."

"So what about Jamison? How does he fit in?"

Murphy scratched his cheek, and shook his head. "I don't know. He knew something and was going to get something for it—near as I can figure. Which doesn't make much sense. But we got some kind of a start, anyway. A way for the crime to happen."

Milt came in. "I put the bodies in the shed in back, Doc, with Old Colonel and Jamison. We got to bury them; they're getting stacked up like cord-wood."

Murphy went to the door and Milt followed. "I'll be down for awhile. You take the town again. I'll need three, four hours, then I'll come back to the office. You go back there and get that Greener and carry it with you. You see something you don't like, you aim for the middle of the biggest part, and pull both triggers." He was still shaken by the incident at the saloon. "Cover yourself."

And he walked, not across to Harry's, but back to Midge's. There were some things to say, and some things to do. He wanted them said and done before things went much further or it was too late.

When he got there Midge was waiting, not in the kitchen where he expected her to be, but in the back, in her room. Murphy walked in, saw her sitting and then saw her stand, holding her hands together in front, framed in the doorway like a picture. Her eyes were red from crying and some hair had come loose and hung across one eye. Murphy reached with his right hand—his left arm was already too stiff to move—and pushed her hair out of the way, around and over the top of her ear. His large hand just brushed the hair back. He leaned forward, put his lips on her lips, and just held that. Not kissing, but touching, knowing each other. Then he pressed a bit harder and held her with his good arm. Her arms came up around his neck and for a time they said nothing.

"When this is done . . ."

"I know. You don't have to say it."

"Yes. I do. When this is done it'll be us. Not just me. But us."

She nodded. He would have said more but she touched him and kissed him. He smiled because there was still some flour on her cheek and there was nothing to say. Nothing to say. Just the curve of the big man over her, smiling.

Nothing to say.

CHAPTER 14

THERE WERE SEVEN of them, the city fathers. Murphy looked at them with barely concealed disgust. They were in the back room of Jensen's dry goods store. Added to the four who had been in the cafe were Jensen, Klein from the barber shop, and Baker, the blacksmith.

"So," Hardesty said, "we're all here. Tell us what you've got." It was always Hardesty, Murphy thought. The banker was always the one who tried to take power, always tried to run a discussion.

"I'd rather not." Murphy was standing, the rest of them sat around a large oak table which Jensen had ordered from the East when he thought he was going to be rich. Murphy looked at Jensen's boot toe in the light but could not see a cut. Of course he could have two pairs of boots. But that was rare in this country. They were stiff when you got them, and most men settled into one pair after they got them broken in.

"It seems to me that we deserve to know what you're doing." Hardesty pushed. That's what he did best, Murphy thought—he pushed. But again there was something else in his voice, in all their eyes. "We pay your wages."

"You hired me. You don't own me. And if you don't like the way I'm doing my job you can sure-as-hell fire me."

"All right, all right. Let's hold it back a little, gentlemen." Jensen slapped the table gently with his right hand. "We're all on edge."

Hardesty smiled, easing down. "I guess it's the tension. What with Jamison getting shot we're all on edge. I just thought that I, that is, we might be able to help if we knew what you were doing." Oily, smooth. The banker talked, Murphy thought, like cooking grease.

"What did you have in mind," Murphy asked, "making up a posse?" He smiled, thinking of a time four years ago. Some men had raised hell and shot up the town. Murphy had called for a posse to go after them and get them back to pay damages. Not one of the men in the room had volunteered. Murphy had gone after the men alone—had caught them in the break country north of Cincherville. They had shot his horse out from under him and left him to walk twenty-seven miles back. Murphy had never said anything to Hardesty or the others, not even when they didn't come to look for him. He had just let it die. But it rankled him. Especially now. "You going to kick ass out here, Hardesty?"

He could see anger in Hardesty's eyes, but the banker backed down again, which didn't make sense. He had never backed down before. This thing was getting them all wonky, fuzzy-headed.

The day had been full of frustration. They buried Sarah Penches at nine in the morning. The whole town had come. It had been pitiful to see the small coffin—children's coffins always looked doubly sad—go into the fresh grave, watch her mother and father throw a handful of dirt on it, and collapse into their friends' arms. Charley went down like he'd been axed. Frustrating to see that, to know the end of Sarah and not have anything to go on.

All day he and Milt had tried to find the rifle or trail of the rifle, find where it had gone. Nothing. Nobody had seen it or heard anything about it. At least nobody yet. A dead trail. A smoke trail.

And after a frustrating, sad day Murphy had to come and face this . . . this gaggle of buzzards.

"The problem, as I see it, is that we have to settle people's nerves about this whole business," Klein put in. "We aren't a big town, but we have people talking about leaving. They're afraid to come outside. My sales are down, way down. People don't want to buy, with something like this in the air. We have to do something to settle them down. Now, if we had something we could tell them, something to show . . ."

He let it hang but Murphy followed easily enough. "I'd still rather not talk about it, about what we are doing."

"But you are doing something?" Hardesty again.

He nodded. "We have some ideas we're following, seeing where they'll lead. Yeah. We're not standing still. Did you think we were?"

Hardesty leaned back, put his fingers together on the table and made a tent. Seemed to think. "Perhaps we are missing something—all of us. We might be overlooking a solution to the problem."

Murphy wasn't going to ask. He waited. Finally Shannon broke the silence. "What are we overlooking?"

Hardesty smiled. "Those two men last night. The ones our sheriff had to handle."

"What about them?" Murphy asked.

"Well, let's suppose, just for the moment, that they were the ones who . . . who did that to Sarah. The ones who killed Jamison and Old Colonel."

"But they weren't," Murphy said.

"Now wait a minute. Just a minute. That's easy to say, but shouldn't we look at this for a little bit and make certain we know what we're saying here?"

"I know what I'm saying." The lamp flickered in the middle of the table as a draft caught it, threw smoke against the shade, and made sudden shadows. "I'm saying those two riders I had to shoot last night had nothing to do with Sarah."

"Can you be sure? Can you be really sure? What if, just for the sake of argument, those two men somehow came to town two days earlier and did . . . Sarah that way." Hardesty paused, a flicker. "Wouldn't that, effectively, solve all our problems?"

Shannon nodded, excited. "I see where you're going with it. Since they're already dead we could spread the word and that would be the end of it. We could get Cincherville back to normal."

Murphy snorted. "But it's not true. And if we do that, the son-of-a-bitch who really did it will still be loose. Think of that. Sure, you might sell more— damn it, that's all you care about, isn't it? How much you bastards can sell?"

"We care about the town, Murphy!" Shannon flared. "This town is being torn apart. If you admit that those two men might have been the ones, that will go a long way to ease tension around here."

"And the fact that it doesn't work has no bearing on it? The fact that it isn't true?"

"But it could be. They were in the saloon talking bad about women, how rough they had been back in the Territories to Indian women. Some of the men heard them. And they were animals. They could have been the ones."

Murphy shook his head. "Hell. Tell them anything you want, but it won't wash. What about Jamison?"

"Maybe he saw them," Shannon said. "It could have been that way. He saw them . . ."

"And then rode out of town without telling anybody, so they could blow him in half?"

Shannon thought a moment. "Well. It's not perfect, but we could get around some of the rough parts. We could make it work if you agreed with us and said they might be the men. Just that—they *might* have been the ones who did that to Sarah."

Murphy shook his head. "You're on your own this time." He was sure now. When this was over he was done. This damned town, he thought. "You're all garbage, you know that. You're something brown on the end of a stick. I'll tell you one thing, one thing right now—we know that Jamison was shot with his own rifle, a bull gun. Whoever has that rifle is the man who took Sarah in the barn. And when I find whoever it is, nothing, nothing in this world will stop me. And it wasn't those two saddle bums."

Murphy turned and slammed out of the door of the dry goods store, breaking one of the panes of glass as he went.

On the street a freight wagon from the McCormick mine had to pull up to keep from running him down as he stomped across the street and into Midge's.

She was closing up for the night, washing in the kitchen when he came in. He walked back to the kitchen, poured himself a cup of coffee from the pot on the stove, and sat at the table, holding the cup silently with white knuckles. "Goddamn town."

"I take it the businessmen's meeting didn't go so well."

"Ahhh." He didn't finish it. He started to tell her about the meeting but dropped it. There wasn't anything to say about it. He sipped the coffee and she poured a cup and sat with him.

"You want to talk small or big?" she asked, smiling. The night before much had passed between them.

"Either way. But sort of short. I have to make rounds pretty soon."

"I figured, as mad as you were, you wouldn't be doing that."

He shrugged. "I'll do the job until I quit. And I won't quit until I've got the man who . . . well. You know."

She nodded. "Is it possible that you're just missing some small part that would make it all make sense?"

"I don't know. I don't know. I mean, how can somebody do that in this small a town and get clean away with it? That's what's got me buffaloed.

You'd think that somebody would have seen it, or heard it—would have seen or heard something."

She nodded. "You'd think so. There must have been noise."

"Milt and I have asked everybody we can think of if they saw or heard anything. It's been a long day. And nothing. Not a sound was heard, nothing unusual was seen."

"At least nothing people remember."

"Right."

"Or you missed somebody."

"Right."

"Are you going to sleep tonight?"

"No. Why do you ask?"

"I just wondered if I should keep the pillow fluffed for you."

He smiled. "Best be careful. You'll spoil me."

He stood, rinsed his cup, kissed Midge good night, and was in the street, halfway back to the where Milt was waiting, when it hit him.

Somebody had seen it, or heard it. Somebody had known about it. Somebody knew enough about what he'd seen that he had to be silenced.

Jamison.

Jamison must have seen it.

But then why ride out of town?

What in hell had he been doing?

There was no lamp going when he got to the office, and Milt wasn't there. It took Murphy two or three minutes of fumbling in the dark to find a match and light the lamp on the desk—a mantle lamp that threw a white light when the mantle worked right.

In the glare of the light he found a note from Milt. The writing was so poor it was barely legible and almost every word was spelled wrong.

"Might have a lead about the rifle," the note read, "went to the McCormick mine. Didn't want to bother you at the meeting. Back tomorrow. Milt."

Damn, Murphy thought. Nothing more than that. Nothing about where the lead came from, what it was—just that.

He thought at once of following the young man. But it was night, and the town would be left without law if he went. Somebody had to be here. He looked to the gun rack and saw that the Greener was gone. Well, that was something. He had enough gun with him.

Murphy took the carry lantern with him, went to the livery, and saw that two horses were gone, a riding bay, which Hodges had once said he favored, and another shag sorrel Old Colonel had bought off a string some ranny was hoping to sell to the army. Somebody else must have taken the shag sorrel, although he couldn't remember seeing anybody ride out. It was strange being in the stable, made his chest tight, and he hurried out. It was a raw place, a torn place full of bad, full of evil.

He blew the lantern out, hung it on a nail, and went into the street.

The town was closed down. The saloon was closed, due to the owner being dead and to the trouble the night before. All the stores were shut down, nothing moving. As he watched the last light in town, the lamp in Midge's window went out.

It was going to be a long night.

CHAPTER 15

NEAR TWO IN the morning Murphy was standing under the wooden awning of the harness shop, which kept the sun from cooking the leather in the display window and ruining the harnesses. There was just the smallest sliver of a new moon starting, and it gave the town a soft glow. Not a light so much as a lessening of the dark. He wished he was in with Midge, curled as he was the night before, with her back against him—and to hell with this. He was thinking of that when he saw movement again, and Clyde came from between two buildings across the street.

At night, he thought. At night the town belongs to the law and the drunks. The law and the drunks and the rats in back of the feed store. That's our town after it closes down.

Clyde was past good drunk and into the puking and falling down stage. He staggered and fell twice trying to get across the street; in the middle he went to his hands and knees and started vomiting.

Have to take him in this time, Murphy thought, watching him. He'll pass out there and a wagon will drive over him in the morning. When Clyde was done throwing up, Murphy walked out and took him by the collar, not without affection. He liked Clyde. Couldn't stand him, but liked him. Clyde was still on his hands and knees. Murphy kicked dirt over the mess—didn't want to offend the citizens in the morning—and hoisted Clyde easily to his feet.

"Who? What?" the drunk mumbled. "Oh—it's Murphy. Old Murphy. It's the law, ain't it? The old law is here."

Murphy could barely understand the words but knew the slur. When Clyde got to the slurring stage he had about half an hour before he dropped. "Come on, Clyde. I'll take you to your room."

Clyde came easily enough, and Murphy half-carried, half-shoved him to the office and jail.

"Old law, help the old law. I'm glad to help the old law."

"Sure, Clyde. You like to help. You help me now by getting into a cell and sleeping."

"No. No! I helped. I'm glad I could help. All I want to do is help. Help . . ."

Murphy put him in a cell, left the door latched but not locked, and went to the front. There was coffee on the stove. But the stove was cold and so was the coffee. He didn't feel like firing it up but was a bit sleepy, so he poured a cold cup and drank it, grimacing. Milt had made it earlier; it was getting to where it could be chewed.

Milt.

What had he run into? Something out at the mine. But what?

Murphy sat at the scarred table, turned the lamp up, took the tablet out of the drawer, and wrote on it. Tried to write everything he knew or thought he knew about what was happening.

Old Colonel was probably drunk, sleeping it off in the loft, and died just because he was there. Died. Without seeing or knowing who had killed him—until the three pitchfork tines slid into his belly; woke to see the face of Sarah's killer; but probably still didn't know why he was being killed.

Jamison had been in the livery and taken the buckskin. He must have. Early that morning. He had taken the buckskin without telling Old Colonel. But that was nothing new. Locals often took rental horses and paid when they got back, if they couldn't find Old Colonel. So Jamison took a horse and rode out of town toward the McCormick mine.

And Hodges had gone to the McCormick mine.

No. Wait! Back to Jamison, first. Jamison saw or thought he saw something, knew something had happened. But rode out of town anyway, without telling what he saw. Why? Jamison was always one for lining his pockets and working on deals to make money. And he didn't care much how he got it. Could this have been some of his greed?

God, with Sarah there in the dirt? Could he have been working some angle like that, trying to make something out of it? And what had he been trying to get? If it was blackmail, then the man he was sticking must have had a lot. Even Jamison wouldn't have ignored what had happened to Sarah without a hell of an inducement. So the man who attacked Sarah must have been worth something.

Maybe.

If Jamison was trying to get something.

But why the McCormick mine?

And it was something at the mine that had drawn Hodges as well.

Something at the mine.

Murphy leaned back and looked at the notebook, juggled what he had written, but still couldn't make it balance. He took a sip of the cold, rancid coffee. Outside he heard coyotes, yapping and working on the dead horse Milt had dragged to the outskirts of town. It sounded like a dozen but was probably only two or three. They made a hell of a racket when they got to feeding and fighting over dead meat.

He turned back to the tablet.

Say this, he thought. Say this—some miner did that to Sarah. God knows there were some rough men at the mine, some rough, pure-D animals, like Shannon had said of the two men Murphy had killed the night before. Or was it two nights? He shook his head to clear it. There were men working mines who should not be with normal people. Mines were rough places to work, and they bred brutal men—savages.

So, say a miner came in to town, caught Sarah in the stable alone, and did that. Then went upstairs and killed Old Colonel. Yeah. Say that. Then Jamison came in and caught him, or saw him.

Then Jamison followed him out of town, bent on revenge or looking to line his pockets from some dirt miner, and got blown up by his own rifle, well off the road to the McCormick mine—where he had no business being at all. The whole damned thing fell apart. Murphy threw the tablet across the room, against the wall. Jamison wouldn't go out on his own to seek revenge, he had nothing to do with Sarah. And no miner would have enough to bribe Jamison to keep quiet about Sarah. Maybe the head of the mine, but he was back East. Only foremen and workers were at the mine itself. It just didn't hold together.

"Oh, hell!"

There was a drunken moan from the cells as a loud noise stirred something in the unconscious Clyde. Then there was silence again, except for the coyotes on the horse. Murphy sat and stared at the wall for a full five minutes, thinking, but nothing came to him. He finally closed his eyes and leaned back in exasperation. He didn't mean to doze, but he was tired and aching from the wound in his shoulder. Sleep took him—the light sleep of night that belonged to the law and the drunks and the rats. Work sleep.

He wasn't sure how long he dozed, but he was awakened by the hacking sound of Clyde throwing up. Murphy got up and opened the door to the cell room. "You came to."

Clyde nodded but got the dry heaves and didn't say anything. The sound made Murphy think of when things were normal. Four, five days ago? Was that it? God.

"I found you crossing the street and down . . ."

"I know." Clyde wiped his mouth with a sleeve that had probably never been washed. "I remember."

"You do?"

"I don't always black out. I remember lots of things."

"You do?"

Clyde nodded, winced with his head movement. He was still drunk, although not nearly as bad as he'd been. "I remember telling you I had helped the law. Did I help?"

"Not much that I know of. What are you talking about?"

"With what I told that kid you got working for you?"

Murphy waited. Clyde had dreams sometimes, dreams about bugs on his arms, snakes, old dead friends, fairy castles in the clouds, and winged serpents. Sometimes they were real but more often they were not. Finally Murphy prodded. "I still don't know what you're talking about."

"That kid . . ."

"Hodges. Milt Hodges."

"Yeah, him. Your deputy. He was asking all over town about that bull gun that belonged to Jamison, but he never asked me. Never asked me. Never asked the old, town drunk."

Murphy waited again. "All right, so I'm asking, damn it. What about the gun?"

"Jamison never fired it. He bought it to hang."

"We know that much."

Clyde had a sharp look in his eyes now. "But did you know that he didn't own the gun more'n about two hours? He sold it right after he bought it off of Charley. Oh, say, ain't it sad about Sarah?" Clyde sometimes shifted time when he was drunk, so that things from the past happened at different times. "Ain't it sad about her? Poor little thing done like that. Oh, ain't it sad?" And he started to cry, leaning back against the wall.

"Who bought the gun, Clyde?"

"Well, I don't know his name, rightly. I don't know who bought the gun." Clyde shrugged, a great drunken lifting of his shoulders, and wiped his eyes. "But he's one of the holers out to the McCormick mine. I was there in the saloon when Jamison sold it to him. I was the only one there. The only one to see it, and you never asked me about it. He said he was going skin hunting in a year or so, but he was drunk and you know how that is. When somebody is drunk they'll say anything. Probably never meant to hunt at all. He was just paid, and you know that Jamison sold the gun for almost twice what he paid Charley for it?"

Murphy waited but Clyde was done. He turned, went back into the cell, and dropped on the iron cot. Done. He would sleep again for hours, passed out and not knowing the world, not knowing anything of the world or the beehive he had tipped over.

A miner had the rifle.

And Hodges had gone out to the McCormick mine.

Murphy blew the lamp out and headed for the livery and his sorrel, at a trot. There were still some unanswered questions, maybe too many, but one thing was certain. Murphy wasn't about to sit and wait for things to come back to him. He would meet Hodges on the way back. If he was coming back.

CHAPTER 16

FOR THE FIRST time in his work as a sheriff Murphy cursed the fact that he was big. Hated his size. He flogged the sorrel out of town with his hat, at a run, making a line southwest as the sun came over the horizon. Blue dawn, blue dawn sky. Once his mother had sung him some kind of lullaby, some drunken lullaby as she put him in the corner box he had for a bed, something from a mother's love. The song, something about a blue dawn sky.

Blue dawn sky,
Blue dawn sky,
Hush my baby,
Don't you cry.

But this dawn was blue cold, blue death sky. The sun cut the sky in the east like a knife, brought a light that hurt. Blue death sky, blue death sky. It

145

was a chant in his head to match the sorrel's driving hooves.

If he had been smaller, the horse would have been able to run faster. Murphy sensed the need for speed. Some part of his brain screamed for speed. This whole thing had been happening one step ahead of him. The killer, the miner, had known what he was going to do, was one jump ahead all along. And Hodges was riding into it. The need to hurry was on him like a fire, driving him—down through his legs into the sorrel—driving Murphy, back straight, hat jammed down, elbows floating— get some, horse, get all the miles there are. What was going to be done would probably be done, whether he hurried or not. But still there was the lunge in him, the hot burn of worry. He urged the horse on, drove him, riding well forward to put his weight on the horse's shoulders, to ease the burden so the horse could carry the weight more easily.

Driving the sorrel, driving him down but not caring, he covered the miles toward the McCormick mine. He would have made it only one way, would have had to leave the sorrel there, at the mine, had he gone all the way.

But when he was five miles out of Cincherville, with the horse covered with sweat and giving steam in the morning cool, he came on the bay that Milt had been riding. The bay was not hurt, but trotting sideways to hold the reins out to the side so he wouldn't step on them. The bay went past Murphy before Murphy could get turned.

Murphy wheeled and went after the horse, but the horse was going home, knew it, and had no desire to turn or be caught. When the sorrel started for the bay, he broke into a flat run, head out to the side and reins streaming in the wind. Running empty and with the sorrel carrying Murphy, the bay could outrun Murphy's horse. So Murphy pulled his sorrel up and turned back toward the mine. He thought, but was not sure, that there had been blood on the horse's neck as he went by. A stain, a blur.

Another mile, using the reins to whip the sorrel, grinding his heels into the sorrel, wishing he had rowelled spurs to rake the sorrel, taking the sorrel down and down, and Murphy came upon Milt.

Milt was in a shallow gully on the left side of the road, crumpled against some rocks, wedged in, facing out. Murphy thought Milt was dead and felt an immense, sinking sadness. Another one, he thought, another pile of death where there used to be a man. Murphy rolled off the sorrel but kept the reins in his hand because there was blood here, blood from that damned bull gun hitting Milt. The smell had the sorrel jumpy. There was nothing to tie the horse to.

He leaned down. There was good light. He could see that Milt's whole upper body was soaked in blood. But the chest rose and fell evenly, not ragged, and Murphy realized that Milt was still alive, that the shot had taken him in the shoulder and made a hell of a hole, but that he was still alive. But for how long?

"Can you hear me, Milt?"

Milt raised his head. A slow nod. A lifetime nod. A nod that cost him his soul.

"I'm going to take you back to town. We have to get you to Doc's. I'm going to put you up on the sorrel, and it's going to hurt, hurt like hell. So, be ready for it. You lost blood, but I think you'll make it."

Another slow nod. Then a whisper. "Wait."

"We have to go quick, Milt. We can't wait."

"Wait." Tight whisper, hot whisper. "Might pass out. Might not come back again. It's Hardesty."

"Hardesty?" Murphy had been pulling Milt's belt to wrap around his shoulder, using the torn bottom of Milt's shirt for a compress. Murphy stopped dead. Not believing. "Hardesty?"

Slow nod. "Jamison sold gun to miner named Meeker. Meeker borrowed money from the bank and Hardesty got the gun on the loan. It's Hardesty." Milt's whisper got hoarse, going down. Milt was going down. "Must have heard that I was coming out here. Waited to shoot me. I didn't see him. Didn't see anything until it hit me."

"That's enough. We have to get you back to town."

The sorrel stood better now than he had under Jamison, but Murphy had trouble getting Milt up. The young man screamed once, a short, high, shrill scream that dissolved into small pants of breath and quiet whimpering. Then Milt was in the saddle and Murphy used a piece of strapping from the saddlebags to tie him in.

Murphy pulled the sorrel to a rock, stood on it, climbed up in back of Milt, holding the wounded man in the saddle, and started back for town, the sorrel weaving with the load.

They made only half a mile. About five miles out of Cincherville, the sorrel staggered and went down on his knees. He was too far gone to make it, ridden too hard to take a double load. Murphy swung off before the horse was all the way down, pushed him back up, and started running. He ran in front for half a mile, stumbling in his boots, but Milt was weaving too much in the saddle to stay without being held, so Murphy dropped back and hung on the horn, running alongside and holding Milt in the saddle with one arm.

Driving the sorrel with curses. Hanging on the side. Thinking now only of wind to breathe and of the word "Hardesty." Hardesty. Paying for every foot, every yard, with his lungs and with the sorrel's life. Murphy hung on the horn and ran.

Twice more the sorrel tried to go down, would have collapsed, but Murphy brought him up, cursing him, kneeing him, and driving him from the side, until at last Murphy saw the buildings—saw the smoke from Midge's stove and thought he would make it—knew he would make it. The sorrel went down.

Murphy felt the horse let go, felt the muscles

relax, and he knew the horse wouldn't be getting up, knew the horse was done. Murphy caught Milt as the horse dropped his head into the dirt. He took Milt, cradled him, and started trotting, carrying him, not thinking at all now, only sensing that he had to get Milt to Doc Hensley.

Staggering, falling forward, Murphy came through town, carrying the unconscious form, until at last he crashed into Doc's office, screaming for Doc to wake up, wake up, damn it, and save this one.

Save this one.

Doc got up, bare from the waist up, pulling his suspenders up—not questioning but going to work immediately. He used his training from the blown and blasted war years, used all of it, knowing speed was all there was. Doc went to work and Murphy went outside thinking:

Hardesty.

Released from the weight of Milt, Murphy felt light, giddy, but still torn down by the run. He had his Smith in his hand now and was going to kill, was going to kill.

Hardesty.

The banker would run now. He would have to run. He would have to know that Murphy would find him, would take him, would kill him. Hardesty would have to run but he wouldn't run without his money. Wouldn't run without that. He loved his money and the power it bought him, too much to leave without that.

Hardesty.

Murphy looked up the street. Nobody had seen him go by with Milt. There were no people out in the morning sun, yet. Still too early. It might be, he thought, it might be Hardesty isn't here. He might not have come back. He might have gone on to the mine to kill the miner. He might have already come, taken his money, and run. A hundred things he might have done. And none of them would save him. None of them would stop Murphy.

Hardesty.

Murphy took four deep breaths and forced himself to be calm, to think.

The livery. He looked across and studied the livery stable. Waited and watched, but saw no movement. He watched the street, saw nothing. Another moment, he studied all of it—the town, the street, the sun—and he studied all that he was. Then he started across the street to the stable, still with the gun in his hand. To kill.

Hardesty.

In the livery Murphy moved sideways and crouched in a holding stall until his eyes got used to the dark. He could see the shag sorrel in a stall, not tied, standing with a saddle still on his back, drenched with sweat. Still glistening and shiny wet with it.

So Hardesty was back.

He was here.

Was he close? Oh, Murphy thought, is he close to

this place now? This place where he killed. Has he come here now, is he waiting for me here?

Murphy moved across the fronts of three stalls, breathing through his mouth silently, watching, waiting. He crouched, his nostrils flared. I can smell him, Murphy thought—I can smell the bastard. What is the smell? Fear?

"Hardesty . . . you here?" Softly, then Murphy moved in the stalls to a different place. "Hardesty. I know it's you. Milt Hodges didn't die. He told me it was you. Talk to me." A whisper. Murphy stood listening, heard nothing, nothing, he was getting ready to leave the stable, then he heard it.

A brushing sound. Hay being stepped on, hay being moved. Across the barn. Murphy started to swing the Smith, had the hammer back and was bringing the barrel up, when the rifle roared.

It was deafening, a thunder of ear-bleeding sound in the small confines of the stable. It filled the center with black smoke. A slug tore through a supporting post, four inches in front of Murphy's face, blowing dust in his eyes, blinding him, but he fired at the sound, four times, as fast as he could, falling to the right, wiping his eyes.

"Give it up, Hardesty. It's done," Murphy yelled, but didn't think he would get an answer. He was surprised to hear Hardesty snort a reply.

"I die, anyway. Maybe I deserve to die."

Murphy knew he was right. He would die, regardless. Either by bullet or by rope. Murphy would kill Hardesty with his hands. Murphy wouldn't be able to stop himself. He lay on his side in the stall and reloaded from his belt, temporarily in good cover. "Why, Hardesty? Why did you do Sarah?" When the Smith was full he got to his feet and, crouching, made his way to the side.

"I can't tell you, not so you could understand. I saw her in the stable. Saw her hair and the curve of her neck. Saw how she would someday be as a woman, as a full woman. The next thing I knew it was done." Hardesty's voice broke. "You think I would have done it if I had known how to stop it? Once it was done I had to kill Old Colonel too."

"What about Jamison?"

"He saw me. Tried to blackmail me. Told me to meet him at the old shack, and he would bring a deed for me to sign. God, what a fool. Then I heard you talk about the rifle and heard from Clyde that he sent your deputy out to the mine. I had to kill Milt. Just like I have to kill you."

Murphy raised the Smith, aimed at the sound, and fired all six rounds as fast as he could pull the trigger. He aimed at the center of the sound and around it, then slid forward and reloaded. All misses, he thought. Then he heard steps running out the back of the barn.

Murphy rose from the stall and cautiously moved to the back door. There were fresh boot tracks heading off to the side, back into town.

To the bank, Murphy thought. Murphy had his back against the wall of the livery stable, looked around the corner, and heard another explosion from the bull gun. This time it was across the street, at the corner by the dry goods store. The cloud of smoke covered half the street. The great slug tore a chunk out of the corner of the barn and went tumbling end over end with a yowling sound.

Murphy saw a piece of cloth across the street and fired three times, but each shot was wild. One of the slugs went to the left of Hardesty by a good foot, through the clapboard wall of the blacksmith shop, and through the bottom of an oil lantern, splashing oil on the forge which was still hot from the evening before. The oil ignited with a woofing sound and quickly spread up the wall of the shop.

Over on the street where the houses were a door opened and closed. People had heard the gunfire but did not come out. Murphy took a quick peek around the corner. He saw yellow flames licking at the roof edge of the blacksmith shop—next to the harness shop—next to the dry goods store—next to the freight office. All of it connected. The rifle thundered again. This time from in between the dry goods store and the harness shop. More people opened doors, but went back when they heard the rifle.

This time Murphy did not fire. Instead, he moved back along the wall of the barn, around the other side, watched the street for a full minute, saw nothing, then ran, loping across the street and around the back of Doc's. Fire consumed the whole smithy and licked at the harness shop. Doc came to his back door and saw Murphy there, watching the backs of the buildings. Doc's hands were covered with blood and he was wiping them on a towel. "Hodges might make it. He's young."

"It's Hardesty," Murphy said, quietly, answering the unasked question, "he's the one."

Doc said nothing but made a low sound. "Do you want help?"

Murphy shook his head. "Stay inside."

"But the fire—it's taking the town."

"Let it burn."

"Murphy." Doc made it soft. Then louder. "Murphy! You can't do that."

"The hell I can't. It's his town. Let the bastard burn."

Doc closed the door and Murphy waited, looking for movement. The fire took the harness shop, hitting the leather oil barrels with dull whumps and spewing flaming oil through the windows into the street and next door, all over the dry goods shop wall. Flames chewed at the oil-soaked dry wood. In two minutes, three at most, the whole side of the street was in flames. Flames worked to the edge of the brick bank. And still Murphy waited. Hardesty would go to the bank. He had to get his money. For him to run without it would be the same as dying. Murphy knew Hardesty would go to the bank. Murphy knew this. This, with the guns and the street and the town. This he knew.

He waited.

It was forty yards to the back door of the bank, a long forty yards, but open and even. Murphy stood, partially in back of the shed on the rear of Doc's house, and watched the back door of the bank.

Hardesty would move there.

Murphy waited and watched and breathed, with his Smith in front of him. Finally Hardesty came for the money. Came to the back door of the bank. The banker crouched near the back wall of the bank, looked around, fumbled in his pocket for the key to the door, and kept his rifle in his left hand. Flames splashed him with bright yellow and smoke gusted past him on the wind.

Hardesty.

Murphy propped his Smith on the side of the shed, eared the hammer back, and shot single action, holding the sights square and even—squeezing first one, then two, three, and four—as fast as he could. Forty yards was a long shot for a handgun, but he held the gun steady and was careful. The first bullet tore into Hardesty's stomach and pushed him upright against the bank wall. He screamed and his rifle went spinning off into the dirt. The second and third shots missed, but the fourth hit his chest.

Then one more hit him as he went down—then one more.

Back out of sight, Murphy reloaded from his belt. Then he turned around and sighted on the downed man. No movement.

Murphy started walking forward, his Smith raised in front of him. Hardesty moved, his leg moved, some last errant command from a dying brain to a dying leg. Murphy put another round into the shattered corpse. The impact took the body back against the wall of the bank into the yellow roar of the fire, into the yellow death-roar of a town dying. Murphy started to reload again when Doc Hensley came to him, put a gentle hand on his arm, and stopped him.

"That's enough."

Murphy turned, his eyes flat—cold gone.

Hensley took the gun. "That's enough."

Murphy shook his head. "No. It isn't."

"Yes. That's all you need to do. You've done enough."

Flames had by now taken nearly one whole side of the main street and were threatening to jump over and take the entire town. People, sensing that the battle was finished, were coming out to fight the fire, but it was past help. The town was gone, Murphy knew. It would cost more to rebuild it than it was worth. The town was dead.

Dead.

He turned to the doctor. "The kid . . . Milt?"

Hensley sighed. His hand was still on Murphy's arm. He removed it. "Milt lost a lot of blood and he should have died on the way in. But he's still alive. I think he might make it, but that arm will bother him for the rest of his life."

Murphy finished reloading. The cylinder turned stiffly because of the powder buildup. He worked it around by hand to free it up. Old habits die hard. Then he put his Smith in his holster. "When I know he's going to make it I'm leaving. I'm taking Midge and I'm leaving." His voice had an edge to it, a challenge, but Hensley didn't fight him on it. "Going to find me some green grass."

And the two men stood in the morning sun, not looking at the body, not looking at each other, not looking at anything.

It was enough.